ACCIDENTS HAPPEN
and Other Stories

Nominations due: January 3, 2025
http://bit.ly/SohoPressIN

Nominations due: February 1, 2025
http://bit.ly/SohoPressLR

ACCIDENTS HAPPEN

and Other Stories

FH BATACAN

SOHO CRIME

Copyright © 2025 by FH Batacan

This is a work of fiction. The characters, dialogue, and incidents depicted are a product of the author's imagination. Any resemblance to actual events or persons, living or dead, is entirely coincidental.

Published by
Soho Press, Inc.
227 W 17th Street
New York, NY 10011

Library of Congress Cataloging-in-Publication Data

ISBN 978-1-64129-511-6
eISBN 978-1-64129-512-3

Interior design by Janine Agro, Soho Press, Inc.

10 9 8 7 6 5 4 3 2 1

Dedication to come

CONTENTS

ACCIDENTS HAPPEN 1

NO. 1 PENCIL 31

DOOR 59 61

THE ONE CRY 89

KEEPING TIME 137

THE GYUTOU 159

PROMISES TO KEEP 175

HARVEST 191

ORIGINAL SIN 201

COMFORTER OF THE AFFLICTED 219

ROAD TRIP 243

ACCIDENTS HAPPEN

Domingo's shift at the wheel began at 8 P.M. and ended at midnight. After this, his partner, Mario, would take over. The refrigerated truck was hauling contraband meat, which had to be taken out of Manila quickly before it could be traced by customs authorities.

Mario had begun to snore loudly in the passenger seat, a loud, rippling sound that came from deep within his throat and nasal passages, filling the cabin and ending with a whistle. The older man glanced at him, suppressed a laugh, and turned his attention to the road again.

The truck rumbled down the expressway—nearly empty on this stretch and at this hour—then sped beneath an overpass.

Something heavy landed on the windshield and a web of hair-thin cracks fanned out from the point of impact. Domingo gripped the steering wheel hard and slammed the brakes, but the huge truck was already shooting down the right shoulder of the road. The wind velocity pressed on the weakened glass, causing it to explode into the cabin in thousands of tiny shards. As he threw up his arms to protect his eyes, he could hear Mario screaming for help.

The left wheels of the truck lifted off the ground as the cargo shifted in its crates to the right side of the compartment. At dizzying speed, the right wheels gouged deep, wide scars in the soft, wet earth of the shoulder. *We're tilting,* Domingo thought, and he yanked Mario toward him, as far away from the impending impact of the crash as humanly possible. He looked out the window and saw only formless black shadows to his right; he hoped they were bushes.

About fifty meters back, not far from the overpass, a black bicycle lay on the shoulder of the road in a knot of twisted metal, its back wheel spinning slowly to a stop.

FRANCIS LOOKS OUT the window of the van, at the other cars on the road, at the industrial buildings looming up on either side, and he feels the familiar sense of dread growing in the pit of his stomach like a living thing. *Home.* Going home again at the end of another school day, a Friday, and tomorrow the beginning of another weekend in hell.

Juanito's walkie-talkie crackles, and a man's voice comes on. It's the team leader in one of the black vans in their convoy. Francis can't fully make out what's being said. After a bit of back-and-forth, Juanito glances up at him through the rearview mirror. "Hey, Francis. Want to stop by Jollibee for a burger or something?"

He wonders why Juanito is always so kind to him, why he always looks at him with such unwanted, unbearable kindness. He burrows deeper into his seat, concentrates fiercely on the traffic outside.

"No." He has to be rude. He can't take kindness just now, not from Juanito, not from anybody.

"It's almost five, and Maring won't have anything ready until past six."

"I said no."

Juanito is like a rubber ball; you fling him away and he just comes right back for more.

"Well, I'm hungry," he says cheerfully. "The boys are stopping at Jollibee. I need to go to the bathroom. Can I get something to eat, too?" They are approaching the restaurant; already Francis can see the big neon sign. He is silent. Juanito keeps on talking. "I think I'll get myself a Champ and a big Coke. And some French fries." He always pronounces the word "French" with an *i* instead of an *e*. And he can never manage to wrap his mouth around the "ch" sound—it always comes out as a "ts": *frints*. Francis wants to laugh but he doesn't, just shoves his hands deeper under his armpits and curls himself up into an even tighter ball in the corner.

Now they are pulling into the parking lot of the fast-food restaurant. Juanito finds a choice spot quickly—it's near the entrance and he'll be able to see the van from inside. He turns neatly into the space, beating a red Toyota Corolla by just a few seconds. He chuckles softly to himself; this is one of the little victories of his small life. Francis wants to chuckle too, but bites down on the urge, bites down hard so that his thin, handsome twelve-year-old face looks old and angry.

The other two vehicles in their convoy find spots not too far away. Juanito turns off the engine, then looks back at Francis. The expression on his face is much less cheery now. "You know, we're not supposed to leave you anywhere unattended."

"I won't be *anywhere*. I'll be right here. In the van."

Juanito sighs. He knows better than to argue with Francis; the boy is always several steps ahead of him. He picks up the walkie-talkie; a few more words are exchanged, an agreement reached. Francis knows the drill. The other men in the convoy—men paid to guard him—will have to take turns keeping a close watch on the van.

Juanito gets out and raps on the glass on Francis's side. When the boy opens the window, Juanito comes closer, shoves his hands in his roomy pants pockets and shakes his change vigorously.

"You sure you don't want anything?"

The boy lets his eyes wander over the parking lot, fiercely ignoring the driver.

"Okay. I won't be long then, hey, Francis?"

He doesn't answer.

As Juanito walks away, Francis's gaze settles on a family with four children, piling out of a small car. Their mother has trouble getting out of the front passenger seat, not only because she is hugely pregnant, but also because the children swarm around her, clamoring for her attention, laughing and babbling and joking. She is able to hold multiple conversations with the children, who cling to various parts of her body and clothes as they move along toward the entrance of the restaurant. They remind Francis of a bunch of ants lifting a morsel of food.

Through the windows to his right, he sees several men

coming up to the van, all wearing dark shirts and sunglasses. All of them are armed, and none of them bother to hide it. That's just how it is. Their leader comes closer to the van, puts his hands up to his face and peers into the windows. Francis tries to make himself smaller in the seat, but it's useless, they know he's in the vehicle. The man walks around the front of the van and Francis is gripped by an irrational fear; he wants to lie flat on the floor beneath his seat and hide. But the door soon opens, and the man sticks his head in.

"Francis?" He's smiling, but not really. He's not like Juanito. There's no kindness in his eyes, no gentleness in his voice, long bled out of them by the life he's lived, the things he's seen and done.

Francis sees his eyes in the mirror, wide and staring; he blinks and then turns away from the man. "Yes." His voice sounds small and frightened to his own ears, and he's almost certain that's how it sounds to the man as well.

"Juanito's inside, yeah." It's meant to be a question, maybe, but it doesn't come out that way.

"He wanted a burger and fries."

"Why didn't you go in with him?"

"He needed the toilet, too. And I wasn't hungry."

The man's other companions have now come to the open door to look in at Francis. They're all of the same physical type: swarthy, thick-bodied and thick-limbed. "Hey, Francis," they say. The boy clenches his fists under his armpits. *Hold the fear, keep it in, don't show them any sign of weakness.*

"Hey." *Steady, steady; they've known you for years, they won't hurt you.*

"Well, we're going in for some food, you want to come along?"

He knows it will be easier for them to keep an eye on him if he comes with them, and he's not about to make it easy. "No, thanks."

The first man reaches in and tries to pat him on the head, but decides the boy is too far back inside. "Okay then, I guess we'll see you at your dad's house later." Not true: two of them will linger around the van, eyes peeled for any irregularity. It's a relief to Francis when the door finally slams shut. He keeps his eyes fixed on the huge Jollibee mascot at the entrance until the other men disappear through it.

It's not long before Juanito comes back with his burger and fries and drink. "Hey." The driver smiles, holding up his packages. "Want something to eat?"

For some reason, he feels both immense relief and anger; he is afraid he will begin to cry soon. He holds it in, holds it all in, crossing his arms over his chest like a dam to keep everything from spilling out.

"What took you so long?"

The driver's face falls, and he lowers the packages. "There were too many people in the line—"

"I don't care. I don't care about the lines, and I don't care about your stupid burger and fries." He's almost spitting out the words. "You're the one who said I shouldn't be left anywhere unattended."

Juanito knows what he's really saying: *I don't like it when you leave me alone with them.* He digs in his pocket for the car keys. "I'm sorry, Francis."

"And I don't care that you're sorry. Just shut up and get me home."

Juanito says nothing the rest of the way. Out of the corner of his eye, Francis sees the driver anxiously glancing into the mirror at him every once in a while. The boy resolutely ignores him.

THE SHORTWAVE RADIO crackled and the voice on the other end sounded distressed, nervous. He spoke too fast, too breathlessly, and Juanito could barely keep up. But he managed to pick out the most important words: Francis, highway, accident, missing, body.

Juanito picked up the call on the car's shortwave and he turned to look at the thin-faced, unsmiling man in the seat behind him, who heard every word.

"Sir?" he asked. His heart was beating so loudly in his ears he was afraid his employer might hear it.

"Turn around then."

"Yes, sir."

FRANCIS'S MOTHER USED to be beautiful. She had a lovely face and an even lovelier figure; he is at the age when a boy is just beginning to notice women's bodies. Now, when he looks at her, he cannot see the fresh-faced, happy girl in the early pictures around the house. Her dazzling smile onstage as she wore that sparkling blue gown, with the diamanté crown on her head and the Miss

Philippines sash over her shoulder. The tears of happiness in her white wedding dress and veil. The pride when she held him as a baby, posing for the camera in the garden, with the sunlight streaming through the trees.

As the years wear on, the pictures change, and she changes in them. The damage starts to show. She smiles less and less, and the smile is forced, then dull, then vacant. Francis can even tell she was crying a few minutes before a photograph was taken. She starts to hunch her shoulders, as though she is slowly folding in on herself.

Now she's a thin, sallow-complexioned woman with dry hair and dark circles under the eyes. She has thin lips that only occasionally break into a crooked smile, and hands that are always fidgeting, always looking for something to do. Francis has heard all the whispers in the household about her, of course: the way the help always know she's using when her bedroom door is locked, the awful, rotten way the room smells when the door finally opens, the way the helpers argue over whose turn it is to clean the room next. The way his father always leaves a wad of cash in a small woven basket on the console in the hallway outside the room, how the cash is sometimes "for emergencies" and sometimes "to keep her happy." The way the cash now has to be replaced faster and faster, while the door now stays locked for longer and longer.

When he enters the house and goes up the stairs to his bedroom, he always looks in the direction of her bedroom first. In the last few months, her bedroom door has almost always been closed. Today is no exception.

Francis has other brothers and sisters, but they are his father's children by other women. Two of his half brothers study in the same school as he; they are older, in junior and senior high school, and have their mother's bigger bones, stockier build, and curly hair. Occasionally they pass each other in the corridors at recess or lunch, but they never speak to one another. The younger of the two will occasionally glare at Francis, but the older one will pull him away, half-bored, half-annoyed, as though Francis is not worth the effort even of a glare. They all share their father's round, deep-set eyes, although he detects in himself a stronger hint of the hardness around his mouth.

Francis notices these things, how his face falls into the same lines as his father's when he catches himself in front of a mirror, in the glass of a shop window.

Francis is a keen observer of life.

He remembers the day when his father took him to see his grandfather for the last time. The former senator had passed his thin face and hawk-like features on to his son. To Francis, it was a frightening glimpse of himself, many years into the future.

The old man sat in his wheelchair, and observed Francis for several minutes with hard, glittering black eyes. His bony wrists and ankles stuck out of the sleeves and legs of his midnight blue pajamas. He'd been unhappy with retirement, unaccustomed to the loss of influence and attention, but he'd made sure his son would carry on the family business, which was, is, and always would be politics. He'd suffered a stroke a few years after, and the imposing figure seemed to have shrunk since. Francis had seen photos of him from the seventies, when he was at the height of his political career, tall, well dressed, handsome. Now, as shrunken and helpless as he was, one tube sticking out of a nostril, another snaking out from under his shirt, neither age nor illness had diminished his coldness and arrogance.

Some food had been served, and some cold pineapple juice in a glass, but Francis had refused. He couldn't bear the thought of eating in front of his grandfather. He could feel somehow that the old man approved of this, that abstinence was some kind of virtue in his eyes.

Instead, Francis sat on his hands, conscious of the paleness of his thin legs against the dark blue of his school shorts. He looked around him, at the books on shelves, the capiz-shell lamps, the large green oxygen tank beside his grandfather's wheelchair. He'd only been to this house a few times before—the old man wasn't sentimental about seeing his grandchildren, though he kept track of them well enough—but it always gave him the creeps. It was old and dark in places, but someone had taken care to polish the wooden floors until they gleamed, reflecting the light from every crack and seam and opening. The sounds from the street outside, traffic, voices, dogs barking, floated up through the windows, but inside there was only silence.

Francis's father came back to the room when it was time to go, and the senator caught him by the wrist.

"Ricardo," he said. His voice was raspy, and the words came out slowly, but there was no mistaking what he was saying. "Keep an eye. On this one. He's. Not like. Your other. Brats." Francis smelled tobacco and decay on the old man's breath when he hesitantly came up to kiss him on the cheek. But he felt strong, thin hands gripping his shoulders and holding him at arm's length, endured the stare of those hard black eyes fringed with white lashes. "You are. A keen observer. You watch. And wait. The best ones. Always do." Then the hands fell away, and the white lashes closed over the eyes. "You'll be. Next."

Next what? Francis didn't want to know, though deep down he already did.

A week later the old man was dead. There was a wake and a big funeral, television crews, lots of important people paying their respects. Or maybe not. Maybe, Francis thought, they were just glad he was finally gone.

Over the years the job of raising Francis had fallen pretty much on the shoulders of Juanito's wife, Maring, who does the cooking and supervises the two younger maids. She is a rather rough, vulgar woman, given to blurting out the crudest terms for male and female genitalia when surprised or irritated. She has a lot on her plate balancing the many demands of the household—particularly the endless stream of his father's visitors, bodyguards, and assorted hangers-on, all of whom must be fed and tanked up with alcohol. Her attentions to Francis consist of mainly feeding him and sending him off to school on time and in clean, well-pressed clothes. She and Juanito have no children, and privately Francis thinks it is just as well. In his mind's eye he sees Juanito with a nicer wife, somebody quieter and more pleasant, someone who doesn't commence screeching at 5 A.M. sharp and nag him constantly about his salary.

WHEN THEY GOT to the scene, the ambulance was about to leave with the two injured men. The boy's father demanded to talk to them. The police held him back; their injuries were not serious, but they did need to get to the hospital at once. Juanito saw his employer's already icy features grow even colder, and he felt sorry for the senior police officer.

"Do you know who I am?"

How could they not know? His face is on the front pages and in the TV news almost every day, nearly as often as the president. "Yes, sir. We're trying to do all we can to find your son."

"Good. Now get out of my way. I need to talk to those men." He brushed past the policemen, who made way for him in mumbling awe and fear. Juanito followed; he was vaguely aware that behind them, two vanloads of his employer's men had arrived. They would get out of their unmarked vehicles and begin throwing their weight around. In their matching flak jackets, they would run around aimlessly but with a kind of authoritative swagger, inspecting the bike, the truck, examining the deep gouges in the soft earth, but seeing nothing.

The boy's father hammered hard on the doors of the ambulance, and the paramedics had no choice but to let him in. Juanito thrust his hands into the pockets of his jeans and waited. In the cold night air, his nostrils picked up the mixed odors of exhaust, disinfectant, and blood. His employer's face registered neither distress nor distaste, only a chilling implacability.

TODAY AT SCHOOL, Francis walks away from a fight, as he always does. He sees no point in standing his ground and playing the hero. There is always some wise guy around the corner who will come at him simply because he is who he is. When your father is alluded to as a criminal in pastoral letters from the Archbishop of Manila, when citizens' groups rally around your home and burn him in effigy, when he is invited to talk shows to explain his side of some controversy or debate to viewers who phone in and call him names, you become a magnet for ridicule and abuse and mockery of every sort. Your classmates will either avoid you or constantly get in your face, your teachers will patronize you or, if the school needs a computer room or uniforms for the basketball team, become very nice and solicitous and concerned about your welfare all of a sudden.

Today's almost-fight is with Choy Guanzon. The priests have him on scholarship; his father was also their student and had spent nearly a decade as a political prisoner. Francis wants to laugh at the ridiculousness of things: how his school is raising little leftists, with all their fathers' prejudices but none of their understanding of the world. It would probably surprise Choy that Francis knows the circumstances of his father's imprisonment, can tell him the charges word for word, recite trial dates. Francis's grandfather had been instrumental in putting him away. There are copies of the investigation and court documents in his dad's office; Francis can pore over them at will when his father is away.

Francis reflects on this as Choy taunts him in the cafeteria, saying that Francis's father is a crook, his mother a drug addict. Francis finds it infinitely amusing that if Choy's father were standing in his son's place, the two of them might actually have a nice, civilized conversation about world politics and history, the fall of communism in Eastern Europe, the crackdown on democracy in the People's Republic of China, the roots of the conflict between the Israelis and the Palestinians.

You'll be. Next.

Instead, he finishes his soft drink, puts his hands in his pockets, and calmly walks away, the other boy's voice ringing shrilly in his ears. He does not argue or raise his fists against boys he considers his inferiors; he cuts them down to size in his mind and is satisfied. There is not much else that a boy as small as Francis can do.

Now he is sitting in the van outside the Senate, with Juanito in the driver's seat. The air conditioning is on full blast; they are waiting to pick up his father for an appointment in Makati. They usually have to wait like this for hours. Francis checks the time on his wristwatch; he will miss feeding the dogs again. He does not like it when he has to share a ride with his father. He never has anything to say to Francis, just glances at him from time to time over the upper rims of his reading glasses, as if to make sure he is behaving. The senator's indifference fills up the confined, air-conditioned space, like a huge rubber raft suddenly inflating inside the van and pressing Francis hard against the windows.

Francis has finished reading his schoolbooks in the dim light of the vehicle. He's getting bored. He watches the driver in the rearview mirror; the man is starting to fall asleep. At the precise moment when the eyelids close, Francis propels himself out of his comfortable seat and halfway over the back of the front seat, shaking Juanito into consciousness.

"Where'd you used to live?"

"Huh?" Juanito blinks once, twice.

"Before you came to work for us, I mean."

"Oh." The driver rubs his eyes. "Lumban, in Laguna. Why?"

"What's it like?"

"Like?" Juanito knits his eyebrows. "It's a nice place. The ladies make good hand embroidery. And you'll never go hungry. Lots of kesong puti and kakanin."

Francis likes sweets and cakes. "What kind?"

"Oh, all sorts. Tamales. Suman. Biko. All the stuff your Tia Maring brings back for your mother after we come home from a visit."

Francis thinks about this for a while. "Don't you ever think about going back?"

Juanito locks his fingers together at the back of his head and leans back in his seat. "Oh, I don't know," he says. "Maring likes it here. Your father pays us well."

"You could start a business. You could make cakes."

The boy's face brightens, and because he sees it brighten so rarely, it seems that much more beautiful to the Juanito. He feels sorry for the boy, but never sorrier than when the boy seems happy, because it hardly ever happens, and only ever for a short time.

"Yeah. Yeah, I could. Start a business with a little capital. Maybe I'll do that. What'll I make, eh Francis? Kesong puti or rice cakes?"

"You'd have to raise cows to get milk for kesong puti."

"Rice cakes, then. Hardly cost you any money starting up." He smiles contentedly, as if that settles things. They fall silent a while, and then the boy clears his throat nervously.

"Do you like the other guys, Juanito?"

"Eh?"

"You know. Ramon and the others."

The driver frowns. As if by instinct, he glances out the window to his right at the two black vans parked alongside theirs. "They're okay, I guess. Haven't had any problems with them so far."

"But you're not like them." The boy says it quietly, but with a kind of authority.

"I don't have to be," Juanito says. "They've got an important job to do. Me, I just drive."

Francis is silent for a while. "Do you ever feel like getting away, Juanito? Like you've outgrown your life?"

Juanito shifts uneasily in his seat. "When you're a grown-up you can't just run away."

"Why not?"

"Because . . ." The driver stops, cranes his neck to look at Francis. "What's all this talk about getting away, hey, kid?" he chides him gently. "You're the man, Francis. You have everything. You have your computer and RCs and your video games. What more could a little guy want?"

Almost immediately Francis withdraws, slumping back in his own seat, crossing his arms over his chest, drawing his knees up close to his arms. He reminds Juanito of a slug that's been sprinkled with salt, curling up on itself to protect its sensitive underside. "Yeah, sure," the boy says, his voice now flat and expressionless, barely above a whisper. "What more could a little guy want?"

THE DRIVER OF the truck said his name was Domingo. He said he didn't see anything; everything was normal until something fell on the windshield, and he spun out of control. No, he didn't know what it was. Could it have been a body? Yes, no, maybe.

He begged the ambulance workers to please get him to the hospital because he had bits of glass in his eyes, and he could feel them grinding into his eyeballs and the inner surfaces of his lids. If he lost his eyesight that'd be the end of him. All he'd ever learned to do for a living was drive trucks and if he couldn't do that, how could he feed his family?

The ambulance couldn't move until Juanito's employer was satisfied that the truck driver had told him everything he knew. All the paramedics could do was to hold the injured man's eyelids open so he wouldn't blink. But sometimes the reflex is just too strong to prevent. By the end of his interrogation Domingo's eyes were like red marbles, streaming blood and tears.

"DON'T HONK," FRANCIS tells Juanito as they turn the corner into the street leading to the house. "Please don't honk the horn."

"I have to, or they won't open the gate."

"Yes, they will. They know we're coming. It's probably open by now anyway. Please don't . . ." But the driver starts honking anyway, and Francis shuts his mouth in a tight line. The van pulls into the long cobblestone driveway and stops under a huge mango tree. The boy takes his books and bags, struggles to slide open the van's heavy door and begins walking wordlessly down the path to the row of piedra china steps leading up to the large, marble-floored front porch.

"Hey," Juanito says, straining to catch up with him. The little figure keeps walking briskly despite the burden of books and bag and lunchbox, deliberately ignoring him. "Listen, Francis, I always honk so they know we're here. So they can open the gate for us. You know that. So what did I do wrong?"

"Go away, Juanito," the boy says fiercely. "You know you're not allowed inside the house."

Juanito stops, peeved. "And you know we have to worry about your safety. We have to get you inside the house quickly, every day, every single time. It's for your own protection."

The small figure stops as well, and his shoulders rise and fall in a sigh. "If you honk, she wakes up."

A twinge of pity right smack in Juanito's chest. "But don't you want her to wake up?"

The boy turns his head to look at the driver, and for the briefest of moments the young face registers pain. Then it disappears, and the eyes narrow, the features harden, and the driver almost recoils at how like his father the boy looks. "No."

Without another word, the boy turns away and walks up the steps. At the fifth step, he stumbles hard, books flying, lunchbox clattering on the stone. He has tripped on one of the large, rectangular piedra china blocks. It had come loose from its mortar months ago, and nobody has remembered to get it fixed yet. He picks himself up and begins gathering up his things.

Juanito walks back to the van. When he starts the engine, he notices that Francis is still standing over the loose block, staring at it as though it holds some secret.

ON THE WAY to the house, the rain started falling, a hard, driving rain that made it difficult to see the road ahead of them. It also made the traffic worse—yes, it could still get worse, Juanito thought to himself. He thought about the boy, dead or dying somewhere in this awful weather. He wanted to weep.

Behind him, the boy's father was busy making and taking calls on his mobile phone. Some of them were about pending bills, committees and subcommittees, hearings, and inquiries. Juanito understood none of these, except that they had to do with his work. There were other calls, to men in the provinces, about cash transfers through rural banks. These calls Juanito preferred not to understand; they had to do with money, and money was a dangerous thing to know anything about.

He did, however, understand one call his employer made, and although he could not completely hear the conversation, he knew the younger woman at the end of the line was being told she could not see his employer at the usual time and place tomorrow night. Something important had come up.

The phone stopped ringing for a while. The two men sat in silence as the traffic came to a standstill.

"Got any kids, Juanito?"

"N-no, sir." The man could never remember the answer, even after four years of paying his wages. "Not yet."

"Good." He leaned back and tilted his head over the back of the seat, letting out a deep sigh. "Kids can be quite troublesome." He put his hands up to his face and held them there for a few moments. Juanito thought he might be crying. But when the phone rang again and he sat up to answer it, the driver saw his eyes were dry.

ON THE WAY to his room, the door of his mother's bedroom opens. She steps out and sees him. Her face lights up and she smiles sweetly, too sweetly, and holds out her arms to him.

"Hi there, how's my baby?" Francis stands still, steeling

himself for her embrace, for her stale breath, the mingled odors of cigarette smoke and urine that cling to her. "How was school today?"

"Okay," he says.

She begins to stroke his face. It takes all the will he can muster not to squirm. "My sweet baby boy, I'm so proud of you. Your papa and I are so proud of you, we talk about you all the time." She looks up at him as though searching for something, and he hates knowing she can find it in his face: traces of his father in the lines of his mouth and jaw and brow, in the shape of his eyes.

You'll. Be. Next.

He hates that the lines blur in her meth-addled brain so that when she kisses him like this, she is actually kissing the man she sees in his face. The kisses become strange and abnormal and insufferable: not a mother's kisses, the hands wandering over his body in unmotherly affection. *Please stop it. I'm not him.* He can no longer help it; he hunches his shoulders and twists away from her clinging arms.

"Okay, sweetheart, I know you want to go off and read your books," she says, her voice shaking, that part of her mind that's still working, that's still his mother, horrified by her actions. "Isn't that right, Francis? My good, smart boy." Francis turns away resolutely, telling himself not to run, that it will hurt her feelings. He lets his legs carry him as fast as they can down the corridor to his room, never quite running.

"I'm so proud of my bright boy."

Her voice drifts into his room after he has closed the door. Someday soon, he will have to lock the door against her, against those hands and those sweet, sick, poisoned kisses. He wants to cry for her, but when the tears come, he cannot spare her any. She eventually stops talking and he hears her bedroom door close. It will remain closed for the rest of the evening, well into the following day.

He wipes his eyes with the sleeve of his uniform and tells himself firmly that all this has nothing to do with him.

When he falls asleep that night, his dreams are filled with long, lean shadows that close around him like a thicket of dead trees. Several times he wakes; after the third or fourth time, he sits up in his bed, bothered and exhausted, and switches on the bedside lamp.

The computer is sitting in the middle of his study table. It is a real workhorse of a machine, his father's twelfth-birthday gift to him, fast and sleek and powerful. Francis uses it for his schoolwork most of the time; sometimes he talks to grown-ups halfway around the world or surfs the internet. Now, at 2 A.M. on a school night, tired from a troubled sleep, he wants to play a game.

VeloCity X is Francis's favorite video game. It simulates a race over a network of roads, and the player's objective is to cause his opponents to drop out of the race by leading them into accidents. Although it may seem like an awful game to create, it is based on sound science—it was originally designed as a road accident simulator by a group of MIT physicists contracted by the American automobile industry. The software calculated weather, road, traffic, and lighting conditions for various types of vehicles at various times of the day.

Since he started playing it a year ago, the boy has gone from the lowest level of skill—driving a ten-wheeler—to the highest, a motorcycle. Now he is able to cause major road accidents involving his computer opponents and beat them to the finish line. He has learned this skill by careful observation, both of the game and of real-life road conditions when he is brought to and from school.

Wrecks interest Francis, and hardly a week goes by without him seeing one on the South Superhighway. He has taken to monitoring the late-night news for the computer graphics depictions of the accidents, to scanning the morning-after newspapers for the occasional diagram illustrating how they took place. Impact velocities, head-on collisions, side collisions, rear-endings, skid marks, body marks—he knows all the words the police and the newspapers use. He knows the statistics, too; shoulder crashes, for example, are less likely to produce fatalities than crashes spanning center islands. Learning the physics of road accidents has enabled him to beat the computer many times.

THE BOY'S MOTHER stood in the doorway, her face pale and newly washed, her hair tied back in a neat ponytail. This was the first time in months that Juanito had actually seen her, and possibly the first time in the last two years he'd seen her looking alert, fully present in the moment. When her husband stepped out of the Benz, she practically leapt down the steps to meet him.

"Have they found him yet? Did you talk to them? What did they say?" The questions spilled out of her in a torrent of anxiety and fear.

Her husband kept going to the door, outpacing her by one or two steps. "We have to wait, Gina."

"Wait for what? Why? Don't they know who you are?"

He paused at the threshold and gave her the look that usually stops her cold. It didn't work this time. "This is your fault." She began to sob. "This is all your fault."

"My fault? I'm busy working all day."

"Working?" She spat out the word. "Working for what? Working for whom? How much more money do you need? How many more people are on your payroll these days?"

"Don't blame this on me. If you weren't drugged out of your mind all the time, he never would have been able to sneak out of the house." He took the stairs to the second floor two at a time, determined to leave her behind, but she scrambled after him, clutching at the back of his suitcoat.

"If you're so hardworking and so honest, why do people talk about us behind our backs? Why does everyone hate you? You're the reason he ran away. You killed him. You killed our son." She almost choked on the last few words.

Their voices faded down the upstairs hallway. The last thing he heard was the father repeating, *Shut up, will you shut up, just shut up* . . .

Juanito turned and began heading back toward the van. On his way down the piedra china steps, he noticed that the loose block Francis had tripped on the other day was missing. He parted some of the low flower bushes on either side of the steps to look for it, but he couldn't find it.

WHEN MARING CLEARS the last of the breakfast dishes away, Francis stands up and follows her to the kitchen. On the kitchen counter are two large metal bowls filled with chunky wet dog food. "Can I give it to them now? Can I?"

"Sure." Maring is busy at the sink and doesn't even look at him. He takes a bowl in each hand and walks carefully to the screen door, kicking it open with his right foot. There are two four-year-old German shepherds near the laundry area. They stand guard seemingly over the large, heavy-duty washing machines, as well as Francis's bike. Because Francis is so small for his age, the dogs seem much bigger. It has taken him nearly two years to get over his fear of them. Maring and the other maids are glad that the boy is more comfortable now. To be sure, they are also glad to have one less chore to deal with, and if their young master is willing to feed the great beasts, then by all means let him do so.

The dogs wag their long, thick tails and do a kind of happy dance when they see him coming with their food. They know to wait until he sets the bowls down in front of them. They don't bark. They know him, his smell, his gentle, tentative touch. They nuzzle him, rubbing their massive heads against his, licking his ears with their long, rough, pink tongues, before turning their attention to the bowls and their first meal of the day.

Francis's house is always heavily guarded. The walls

around the compound are high. There are two gates, one in front and another on the left side. The security guards change shifts every eight hours. The black vans also patrol the streets around the house, once every half hour, although lately they've grown quite slack, sometimes allowing a full hour or two to pass before going around the house.

To an intruder wanting to come in, the laundry area, guarded by these huge animals, would seem to be the most protected part of the compound. To someone wanting to get out, however, this was the perfect place from which to make an exit without being seen: up the washing machines, onto the roofs of the dog cages, up to the top of the high wall, into the sturdy branches of a nearby tree, a quick climb down to the sidewalk.

"Francis, you'll be late for school!" Maring shrieks, startling him. "Get moving, boy!" He runs back into the house, washes his hands in the kitchen sink, and bounds up the stairs into his bedroom for his books, bags, and his favorite jacket.

A TELEVISION NEWS crew dropped by the house at around 3 A.M. They waited in the sitting room for about half an hour, the cameraman setting up his tripod and lights, rearranging the furniture and framing the shot. Juanito smoked a cigarette and watched them from the garden, through the French windows.

When Francis's father came down, his eyes were rimmed with red, and his usually immaculately styled hair was sticking up as though he had run his fingers through it several times before facing the news crew. He looked terribly tired and worried. The reporter was a pretty young thing in a tight lavender sweater set that highlighted her curves. She leaned in close with her microphone and her lustrous, salon-perfect hair and her eyes filled with compassion and sublimated desire. This poor man. This poor, sexy, powerful man.

Juanito dropped his cigarette on the gravel path in front of him and crushed it savagely with the toe of his shoe. *He's good*, he thinks. *So very good at this.* He hawked up a glob of phlegm from the back of his throat and spat it straight onto the glass of the windows.

IT'S BEEN NEARLY six weeks, but the boy's body has not yet been found. The only thing the authorities managed to recover was his jacket. It was caught on the front wheel of a passenger bus going to Laguna.

Juanito stands at the shoulder of the highway, near the spot where Francis's bike landed. There's a slight drizzle but he doesn't mind. The glare from the headlights of oncoming cars blinds him temporarily and he turns away with a grimace.

This is what the police believe: The boy had somehow slipped out of the family compound, and then out of the gated village undetected, to go joyriding on his bike. He might have gotten lost and wandered onto the more dangerous stretches of the highway. There, he was hit by an as-yet-unidentified vehicle. The impact had caused his body to be flung against the windshield of the truck Domingo Llanes was driving.

Domingo lost control of the vehicle. It was lucky there were no other vehicles close enough on the road for him to hit. But the Laguna bus must have come along a few minutes later and dragged the boy's body under the wheels. His remains would have fallen away after a while.

The police have alerted other precincts along the route, to keep an eye out for the body of a twelve-year-old boy. Juanito had seen the jacket; it was in shreds, smeared with blood and caked with dirt. The boy's father took one look at it, and his mouth tightened in the way it always did when he was angry or upset. He didn't say a word, just nodded to the investigating officer that it was, indeed, Francis's jacket, and then turned away.

This morning the boy's mother packed a few bags and left. Maring said the woman was going back to her parents' home, and then afterward to the US. They don't know it yet, but she's never coming back.

Juanito stands in the drizzle, staring down the highway as cars zoom past him to destinations unknown: Cavite, Laguna, Batangas. To quiet little towns where life is slow and pleasant, and everything shuts down at 7 P.M. He thinks about Lumban, his own hometown, about childhood breakfasts of hot pan de sal fresh from the neighborhood bakery, and leftover local cheese fried crisp in a pan, and scalding hot local chocolate. Farther on, the port in Batangas, the ferries that bring passengers and truckloads of farm produce to Mindoro, to Masbate, to other places he has never seen and probably will never see.

He thinks about all the places he would go if he could,

if he could run away like a child who has outgrown his life. He thinks about these places and hopes that they are kind, welcoming, hospitable. He hopes that at least one of these places holds the kind of peace necessary for a child to grow up happy, or at the very least, safe.

Juanito hopes these things because he himself is a keen observer of life. Because he knows children: how resourceful, how relentless, how remorseless they can be. Because he knows they can plan and scheme and calculate, just like grown-ups, to survive in a grown-up world.

Because he knows something even the boy's own father and mother do not know.

Francis has never learned how to ride a bike.

NO. 1 PENCIL

When Galvez and I pull up in front of the house in La Vista, Mrs. del Mundo's son is waiting for us at the gate. He is about nineteen or twenty, with a round, shiny face. Not very tall, but heavy, well over two hundred pounds of fat and muscle. He is pacing, smoking furiously; the collared gray T-shirt he is wearing is stained in the back and under the arms with sweat.

"What took you so long?" he asks, and I am surprised at the thin, whining voice that comes out of that big body.

Galvez scowls at him. "Where is she?"

He takes a deep drag off his cigarette and throws the stub into the bushes nearby. "I can't go back in there."

We find Mrs. del Mundo at the foot of the stairs, her legs splayed up over the bottom four steps, her neck twisted. There is a broken glass and spilled water all along the right side of the body.

The girl is sitting on the floor in a dark, narrow, musty room beneath the stairs, her knees tucked under her chin. She blinks when Galvez switches the lights on, but she doesn't look at us, doesn't react to us at all. For a moment I think the room is a closet, but there is a small bed at the far end. I would hate to have to sleep in here.

"Shit," Galvez says, "it's hot in here."

"What's that smell?" I ask.

Galvez raises his head carefully, so it won't hit the low, sloping ceiling, sniffing the air. "Piss." He casts a hard glare at the girl, at her faded housedress and disheveled hair. "Somebody didn't make it to the bathroom in time."

I bend down beside the girl. "Come on. Let's go outside." I tap her on the shoulder, half expecting her to lash out, but she doesn't. She comes quietly with us, not even glancing down at the body as we pass it on the way to the door.

The woman's son bounds up across the driveway to meet us. "You little demon," he squeals, and before Galvez can stop him, he lands a stinging slap across her face.

"Back off," Galvez barks. "Back off, or I'll arrest you, too."

I look at the girl. Her left cheek is reddening. It occurs to me that she didn't flinch or try to evade the slap. Her expression hasn't changed at all.

Mrs. del Mundo's funeral is held three days later. Nobody from her deceased husband's family comes, and only a handful of her own relatives bothers to accompany the coffin to the cemetery. They all stand around uncomfortably as the priest delivers the blessing for the dead, and they are all walking briskly to their cars even before the coffin is completely lowered into the ground. That tells me something about her, something incongruous with her son's insistence that she was a good, kind, gentle woman.

She was, by all accounts, a young forty-three; the family pictures show an attractive woman who'd kept her looks, although a certain coldness in the downturned corners of the mouth, in the arch of an eyebrow, spoiled them. Her son swears the girl—his stepsister—pushed her down the stairs. But he didn't see it happen. I have no witnesses, no motive, and therefore, no case against the girl. For now.

THE SOCIAL WORKERS at juvenile hall have been unable to get the girl to talk. Isabel—Isa—is about fifteen, maybe sixteen. They think she might have a learning disability, but I'm not convinced. I've been a police officer for sixteen years. Senior Police Officer 4 Mike Rueda, it says on the roster. Most cops don't get smarter about anything but graft in sixteen years. I guess I'm one of the luckier ones; I'm good at what I do, which is homicide.

Juvenile is a lousy place to be. Wherever you go, it always smells of unwashed bodies and stale food, boiled down to a tasteless mush. This is a girls' facility, though, and better than most, despite the dingy walls and the institutional gray flooring. She is isolated in a small room down the hall from the clinic most of the day. She clearly does not belong here, and something about her—her clean, good looks, maybe, or her silent compliance—strikes a sympathetic chord with the social workers, who are used to tough-talking, glue-sniffing junior criminals.

All day long she sits by a window and taps her right foot to the beat of silent, faraway music. She never speaks, never makes a sound. She looks through us, as though we aren't there.

My partner and I need to talk to the del Mundos' neighbors in La Vista, to get a feel of what the family situation was like. People usually have a pretty good handle on what goes on behind their neighbors' walls and fences, no matter how thick or how high.

But getting Galvez's butt into the field is one of the hardest things in the world, especially on a day as hot as this. I spend the better part of the morning wheedling, threatening, and cajoling him to join me.

The thing that finally gets him is the prospect of meeting some of the neighborhood's housemaids.

Galvez likes house help and waitresses a lot, and they seem to like him back. He's had four or five children by as many women, aside from the four he already has with his real wife. Now, I'm no looker—short, wiry, and so ugly my in-laws still say my wife wasn't thinking straight when she married me. But beside Galvez, with his leathery brown skin and salt-and-pepper hair and toad-like physique, I think I look okay. So his attractiveness to the opposite sex baffles me. I wish I could say it's the uniform, but we don't wear uniforms anymore since we both started working on homicide investigations. It must be something else.

The helper at the gate of the first house we call on is no exception. A shy, plump, toothy girl with round eyes, she takes one look at Galvez and goes to jelly, smiling too much and twisting her fingers this way and that. She lets us in after consulting with the lady of the house, Mrs. Mallari, and asks us to sit on the lawn chairs while her employer gets ready to talk to us.

She disappears into the house a few minutes. When she comes around again to ask us, "Would you like some juice or something?" Galvez stirs ever so slightly in his seat, shifting his pelvis—along with his potbelly—in her direction, and answers with a meaningful lift of the eyebrow.

"Yes, I'd like—something."

The answer causes her to blush beet red from hairline to neck. When she heads back to the house, giggling, he turns to me and gives me that some-guys-have-all-the-luck smile of his. I don't return it.

Mrs. Mallari emerges from her room a few moments later. She is a large, gregarious woman, with bottle-dyed hair piled high on the top of her head. Unlike her maid, she does not give Galvez a second look. When I introduce myself, she grips my hand and shakes it vigorously. She sits in the chair nearest to mine, then immediately begins flapping the front of her red batik caftan to fan herself. The heat, even in the middle of her lush green garden, is oppressive. I like her almost at once, and from the way she looks at me—kind but focused on the business at hand—I can tell she likes me as well. It is the kind of rapport one always hopes for when making inquiries of this sort; the people who like you will almost always give you quality information.

She tells me that Isa's mother Ruth died shortly after giving birth to her. It took Andy del Mundo several years to get over his young wife's death, years in which he raised a quiet, sensitive child. Andy del Mundo married Araceli Robles when Isa was six or seven; she had worked for his small consulting practice and was a widow with a son. "Andy used to worry that Isa could not seem to get along with them."

I lean forward, my elbows on my knees, fingers knotted together. "Was she a difficult child?"

"Oh, no, not at all, quite the opposite. Very quiet, always kept to herself. I think Cely—Mrs. del Mundo—would have preferred a more normal child, you know, noisy, active. Like Alvin."

The maid comes out bearing a tray with glasses and a pitcher of what looks like iced tea with calamansi. Galvez stands gallantly, as if ready to help her with the tray; he's long checked out of the discussion with Mrs. Mallari and is eager for a distraction.

"Mrs. Mallari, I was wondering. Is Isa—delayed? You know. Slow."

She waits for the maid to set the tray down, then pours some of the tea for herself and us before continuing. "You know, we always thought so. Ruth died giving birth to her . . . we thought there might have been complications, but Andy didn't like to talk about Ruth. I don't think he ever really got over her death." She takes a sip from her glass and chews on her lower lip a while. "She looks normal enough, no? But she does move slowly, and she hardly talks. She might be developmentally delayed, although I think she went to UPIS for a while."

I think about this, looking down at the calamansi pulp floating on the surface of my iced tea. Out of the corner of my eye I can see Galvez putting the moves on the girl, who has lingered, hovering around him attentively. He is asking her questions totally unrelated to the case in the low, hot-shit voice he always uses on maids.

As Mrs. Mallari talks, I begin to get a clearer picture of Isa del Mundo's life after her father's death. "Cely was a screamer," she says. "I used to think she must have had a thyroid problem, such a loud woman, so high-strung. She screamed at the dogs, the bill collectors, everyone and everything." She stops for a moment, then adds thoughtfully, "But at Isa most of all."

The stepbrother Alvin was just as bad. Mrs. Mallari describes him as a spoiled young man, arrogant and entitled. He drives around the area too fast, pelts his neighbors' pet dogs with stones, picks fights.

I think about all this for a while; so far, my initial impressions, of the dead woman and her son, of the atmosphere in the del Mundo household, have been confirmed. But nothing I've heard is a sufficient motive for murder. I realize, though, that I am talking from my own point of view; my wife's mother sounds a lot like Cely del Mundo, and to be sure there are days when I'd like to kill her, but that's just talk. I turn to Mrs. Mallari and begin taking my leave. She promises to call me if she remembers anything.

I have to clear my throat several times before Galvez takes the hint.

Mrs. Mallari is looking sternly at her housemaid, and the girl wilts under her mistress's stare. But Galvez not only winks at the girl, but at Mrs. Mallari as well, as I drag him out of the compound by the arm.

Before the day is over, I've been given two more cases to investigate. It's always like this; the new cases pile up before I've had time to make a real start on the ones before them. I could complain, but who listens? These latest are the usual gangland salvage-type killings—two more to add to the pile of similar cases that I already have on my plate, two more I know I won't be able to solve. It's quite likely the guys behind them are down the hall from me, at the anti-narcotics unit. They have their own methods, simultaneously lazy and brutal, of solving the city's drug problems. And they like it when I stay off their turf.

When I get home, the kids are asleep. Dinner was pinakbet done just the way I like it, with a lot of squash and eggplant, the sauce dense with crushed tomatoes and shrimp fry—and I know my wife is upset because the leftovers are already in the refrigerator, my place setting back on the cutlery tray and the plate rack.

As I settle in the rickety armchair in front of the television and peel my sweaty socks off, the thing that nags me most about the day's inquiries in La Vista is how everyone who knew Cely del Mundo said she was a loud woman. They said she would be yelling and screaming from sunup to sundown—at the paper boy who came with the dailies at seven o'clock sharp every morning, at the family dogs, at the succession of housemaids, none of whom could last beyond three months. She reserved her most venomous tirades for the slow, uncommunicative Isa, who apparently was so clumsy and uncoordinated that she had to be moved to the tiny room on the ground floor where we found her that night.

UPIS—the UP Integrated School in Diliman. It's been a long day and I can hardly keep my eyes open. Going to the school in the morning is the last thought on my mind before I finally give in to sleep.

WHEN I GET there, I am told that Isa del Mundo was a student until around the age of twelve; she was pulled out in her final year of primary school with no explanation from her stepmother. Her records show an indifferent student, with below average to average grades in every subject.

When I get to juvenile, the administrator tells me the girl has a visitor. "A teacher," she says.

"A teacher," I repeat. "Why wasn't I told?"

She wrings her hands; worry lines crease her forehead. "I didn't think there would be a problem."

"Hmmm," is all I say, and accompany her to the visiting area. The dingy, pale-green door has a glass viewing panel set in it at eye level; I look in and motion for her not to open the door. She waits by my side a few seconds and then excuses herself.

The two of them are sitting on opposite sides of a dull beige desk—Isa, hair tied back, wearing a loose, faded green top with matching trousers; the teacher, an elderly man in his mid to late sixties. The slip of paper on the administrator's desk said his name was Manuel Arias. He's a small man, fair-skinned, with graying hair and skin grown slack over the fine bones of his face.

It's his hands that catch my attention, so big they look like they have been grafted onto his wrists from a much bigger person's body, the fingers somehow elegant despite being so knotty. He is tapping one long forefinger on the desk and talking. The girl watches him intently for a few seconds, then bends her head to doodle on the surface of the desk with a yellow pencil.

To his left, on the desk, is a small pile of apple and tangerine peelings. He has obviously brought her some fruit and taken the trouble to peel it for her. I'm touched by this. It is the same little pile on the table at breakfast at home, when I peel fruit for the kids, although I haven't done that in a while. By Isa's right hand, a few slices of tangerine lie on a square of tissue paper.

The tapping and doodling, tapping and doodling continue for about five minutes. The girl's face is animated for the first time since I have seen it. She smiles, she talks, her wide dark eyes are bright with interest. I wonder what kind of teacher he is; did he teach at UPIS? Why didn't I see him there?

I hear the tapping of heels behind me. The administrator is back with two attendants. I raise my hand, motioning for them to wait.

She ignores me. "Visiting hours are over," she says, brushing past me.

Arias's face darkens in helpless fury when the door opens. The girl slips back easily into docile blankness. She allows the pencil to slide from her hand onto the desk and stands obediently when the attendants come to take her away. When the women leave the room, I'm left alone with the old man; his anger, barely contained in his tiny frame, crackles through the air in this stuffy room like static.

"Rueda?"

"That's me."

The eyes narrow. "Your report says she might have some sort of developmental delay."

I lift an eyebrow. "You read my report?" Clearly, the administrator has been careless with the papers on her desk.

"I suppose you are qualified to make that sort of assessment," he says, as he sweeps the peelings with one huge, veined hand into his brown paper sack and folds it up. He walks slowly to the door, turns the knob, and is halfway through it when he turns back and looks at me. "You *are* qualified, aren't you?"

I am about to say something when the door opens wider, and Galvez struts in, belly first.

"Oy, pare, I've been assigned to the new salvagings full-time, I need your reports."

The old man takes advantage of Galvez's intrusion to slip out the door. I try to follow him but waste precious seconds trying to get past my lumbering partner before he finally stands aside to allow me to pass. By the time I get to the end of the corridor, the old man has disappeared. Exasperated, I stride back to the visiting area. Because Galvez is incapable of writing a decent report, I've lost a perfectly good opportunity to talk to the old man.

"Next time you need anything from me, Galvez, wait until I get to the office."

The bastard is busy chewing on the slices of tangerine that Isa left uneaten on the table. "What's your problem?" he asks with his mouth full.

I shake my head and sigh. "Never mind." I stand beside

the table for a few minutes, in the place where Isa was sitting only a few moments ago. She left the yellow pencil where it is lying now, and I pick it up, thinking to get back to the office. And then I see it.

On the beige paint of the desk, she has drawn a series of lines, and in those lines, a series of dots and squiggles.

It looks a lot like music.

I'VE MET MANY reporters in my line of work and all of them think they're God's gift to journalism. Joanna Bonifacio is no exception, but unlike the rest of the pack, there's an actual brain ticking under that skull. She's covered Malacañang Palace, the military beat, Makati's swanky bars and boardrooms, and now, for some reason, she's covering crime for the *Philippines Observer*. I think she's just bored and looking for cheap thrills, and there are plenty of those on the police beat.

I ring up her desk at the *Observer* and this low, honey-and-gravel voice—sort of like a female impersonator—says, "Bonifacio." No first name. I can hear the fast, almost aggressive clacking of a computer keyboard at the other end.

"Joe, Mike Rueda from CPD." I try to sound friendly, no hidden agendas.

"Oy." There is a short pause for what I guess to be a sip of scalding coffee. "S-P-O-Four," she resumes. "What have I done to deserve this?"

I clear my throat. "Joe, I need to ask you something. Do you remember that priest friend of yours? The one who helped the NBI with the Payatas killings last year?"

The rapid clacking continues; she must type at over a hundred words per minute. "Yep, Gus Saenz. What do you need him for?"

I try to ignore the question. "Do you know where I can get in touch with him?"

"About what?"

I try not to sigh. "I need his help on a case."

"No kidding."

"He's a musician, right?"

She snickers. "What, you want to invite him to a karaoke joint? I don't think you're his type."

"Come on, Joe. I really need his help."

The clack of the keys stops, and I hear something creaking, possibly the springs of a swivel chair as she drags it closer to the phone. "If I put in a good word for you, will you give me the story?" She tries to sound nonchalant, but I recognize that undertone of interest and excitement in her voice. I hesitate a second or two, but that's long enough for the springs to creak again, and the clacking to start up. "Well, hey, it's been nice catching up with you, but I have to get back to work."

"Okay, okay," I say. "You'll get your story. But I have to warn you, there's a minor involved."

"You're the best, S-P-O-Four," she crows. "Give me an hour to set something up for you."

FATHER AUGUSTO SAENZ is a Jesuit priest who teaches anthropology at the Ateneo de Manila. He is also one of the country's few forensic anthropologists. I have seen him a handful of times on television, helping the police and the NBI on one case or another, but nothing prepares me for the sight of him in real life: movie-star handsome and over six feet tall, with large hands and long legs. He looks much younger than the fifty-odd years I believe him to be. He doesn't even dress like a priest, wearing faded black jeans and a gray linen shirt with the sleeves rolled up to his elbows. When he appears in the doorway of juvenile and walks past the reception desk toward me, the female duty officer and the receptionist follow him with their eyes, their mouths hanging open. I allow him to pass ahead of me into the corridor, then turn to the girls sternly.

"Sunday confession for both of you," I hiss at them in jest, and they titter nervously as they get back to work.

I half run to keep up with him as he heads toward the room where Arias visited Isa. "Thank you for coming down, Father Saenz."

"No thanks necessary." Hands thrust deep into the pockets of his jeans, he walks in long, easy strides. "Joanna said you needed some help. Although I have to admit the police have never asked me to help with a musical problem before."

"No, I guess not, Father. These are—unusual circumstances."

"Yes, she told me. The young girl." He pauses a while, then continues. "I don't recall ever having met you before, and Joanna says she doesn't remember telling you I used to be a musician." He says this matter-of-factly, not really expecting an answer, although I feel obliged to give him one just the same.

"When I was a young police officer, I rode armed escort for Mayor Daniel Rodriguez." He frowns and tries to remember. "You were at one of his parties once," I say. "1984 or '85? You conducted the choir."

"One of his wife's charity things. That was a long time ago, though. I can't believe you still remember me."

Not like you're easy to forget, I say in my head. "Mrs. Rodriguez had a big crush on you. Everyone in the escort knew it."

He stops right before the door of the visiting area and turns to me. His eyes, their irises a curious shade of a color I can't name, narrow. For a moment I think I've said something to offend him, and I'm relieved when he chuckles.

"She did, too," he says, "the old cow!"

I lead him into the room with the desk. "Over there."

Saenz moves away from me, toward the desk, and bends down to examine the writing on the wooden surface. "It's music, all right."

"Great. Can you, uh, read it?"

He sits, and I sit on the opposite side of the desk. I watch as he traces the dots and squiggles down the lines with his forefinger, as his lips move in short, pulsing bursts of air as though to keep time. He does this for what seems like a very long time, and then he goes back to the beginning of the lines and repeats the process.

When he comes to the end, he closes his eyes and begins to hum. I can't understand the music—at some points it begins to make sense, and then he breaks off and follows another line of melody, breaks off again. His face, with the eyelids shut tight, is aglow with pleasure. I realize, of course, that I'm not hearing it the way he is hearing it in his head, and I sit patiently until he is finished.

When he opens his eyes, he is beaming. "Bach."

"Huh?"

"Johann Sebastian Bach. The Allemande from the Suite in E Minor, arranged for classical guitar."

I haven't the faintest idea. "So you've heard it before?" I ask.

"I've played it before. You say this Arias is her teacher? Did you find out what kind of teacher?"

"I guess—"

"Don't guess. Is his first name Manuel?"

I fish out my notebook from my pocket and flip through the pages. "Yeah, that's him."

The priest rocks back and forth in his seat, biting his lower lip, with one eye closed and looking at me out of the other. "Manuel Arias is one of the country's leading classical guitarists." He stands up and begins to slap his thighs with both hands, and I think the movement mimics what's going on in that brain of his. "I don't think your suspect is retarded, Mike."

WHEN THE GIRL is brought in, the guitar is already propped up on a metal stand; Saenz is sitting beside it with his arms folded across his chest. She goes straight to her chair near the window, ignoring them. Saenz looks at me, unfolds his arms and takes up the guitar. He begins to play, quietly. I've never heard music like this before: it sounds like—and this is stupid, I don't know what I'm talking about—like a dream of water and hands and infinite sadness.

The girl does not react. She continues staring out the window, at the yellow-green, paddle-like leaves of a talisay tree. When the music is finished, Saenz looks up at her, then at me. I open my hands and shrug.

Behind me, the door opens and an attendant comes in carrying a tray with a glass of water and two cups of coffee. She puts the tray down on the table and walks out of the room, but unexpectedly, she allows the door to slam shut and I jump, as does Saenz. Slightly embarrassed, I stand, shaking my head, and close it gently.

And then I realize the priest has not taken his eyes off the girl.

"Did you see that?" he asks.

Nothing's changed, as far as I can tell. The girl remains still, closed off to us, the faded green top stretched across her back like a wall to keep us out.

"When the door slammed. You and I were both quite surprised, but she barely reacted." He walks toward a far corner of the room and claps his hands once. She doesn't move, doesn't respond. Then, he moves closer to her, where she can't see him, and claps his hands again. Only then does she turn her head slightly.

"I think you'd better have her hearing checked."

• • •

THE CHROME-PLATED CLOCK on my desk says it's 8 A.M. In reality, it's about ten thirty. Yesterday, Galvez took me through one of those song-and-dance routines he does when he's trying to get me to do his paperwork for him. He came in smoking and talking a load of rapid-fire nonsense about how he's really more of an "action man" than I am, and since I'm kind of a "thinking guy," I'm ideally suited to the job of filling out reports. Without so much as a by-your-leave, he picked up the clock, shook out the batteries and replaced them with failing ones from his battered Walkman. It's now stopped completely. But hey, just one more thing in this place that doesn't do what it's supposed to. Sometimes I wonder if I can apply for a change of partner; better yet, I wonder if the guys at anti-narcotics would be willing to get him off my back for a small fee.

Saenz has picked up Arias from the UP College of Music. We agreed at our last meeting that the old man might be more cooperative if he was brought in by someone who wasn't a cop. When they arrive, the old man looks sullen, and does not take the hand I offer him. He sits in the chair opposite me and looks down at the huge hands resting in his lap.

"You can help her, you know."

He is quite feisty and temperamental for such a little guy. One of the massive hands flies up, the forefinger stabbing the air in my direction. "You want to prove she killed that woman."

"I want to know the truth."

All at once he is a little old man again, and he slumps

back in his seat, looking tired and defeated. Nobody moves or says anything for a while.

"Her father started her on guitar lessons when she was six. I have been teaching over forty years. I have never seen anything like this child. A musical genius. She can play by ear and by sight, she has perfect pitch. She can hear the music in her head as she reads it on the page." He looks from me to Saenz, and back. "You've visited her old school?" he asks.

"Yes."

"Then you've seen her grades. Lousy, every last one. But she is an incredible musician."

The tapping and doodling now make sense; she was writing the notes and tapping them out. "Did she ever tell you what it was like at home?"

The old man's face darkens again. "At first it was difficult to believe. Mrs. del Mundo was always such a charming woman. Very friendly. But at home she apparently tormented that child so. Ranting and screaming from sunup to sundown. The child couldn't do anything right. Do you know she would cry at the end of her lessons? Because she had no choice but to go home to that house, to that constant barrage of abuse." The old man turns to me. "Did they tell you why she was taken out of school when she was twelve?"

I shake my head. "They said there was no explanation from Mrs. del Mundo."

"Of course not. A better place to look would be St. Luke's. Isa wasn't always deaf. When she was ten, she was admitted there for injuries to both ears."

I'm bracing myself for the worst. "You think she was beaten?"

When he looks at me, his eyes hold both profound sadness and gentle reproach. "You are a policeman, Mr. Rueda. You of all people should know how the world works. Haven't you learned by now that there is more than one way to beat a child?"

DR. MAGGIE PATERNO was the otolaryngologist who took care of Isa when she was admitted to St. Luke's. She described the injury to the girl's eardrums as permanent and irreparable. They were punctured, she said, with a No. 1 pencil.

The injuries were self-inflicted.

When I step out of St. Luke's, in the blazing hot sun, with the traffic on E. Rodriguez and the ripples of heat rising from the vehicles' bodies, I feel a pain in my chest that I can't explain. I flag down a cab to get to juvenile, and the pain just sits there, bearing down on my chest from outside, or straining it from the inside, I can't tell. I think about what I have just found out, think about both the desperation and the fierce courage it takes to drive a pencil through your eardrums so you can silence the world, think about how I'll probably never write with a pencil again. I think and then it all becomes too much for me; the cab driver, handing me a box of Kleenex from his dashboard, asks if someone has died in my family.

At juvenile, I ask to see the girl.

In her room near the clinic, Saenz's guitar is still in its

stand; he's been hoping to reach her through it. She is sitting by the window in her usual place, staring at the talisay tree. She doesn't mind me; she never has and she's unlikely to start now. My head hurts and I'm tired. When I get out of here, I'll still have a bunch of cases to look at. I haven't been home early enough to play with my kids in the last two weeks; by the time I get back, they're already asleep in their beds.

Stress and frustration are a regular part of my life, but right now, I'm just fed up with it all, and the girl, with her blank face and staring eyes, is a convenient target for my bad humor.

"Talk to me, damn it. I'm trying to help you."

Of course, she doesn't. She just sits there.

I lean forward and rest my elbows on my knees, close my eyes, open my hands, and press the heels of the palms against my eyelids. The action relieves the pressure there, but not much. The inside of my brain swirls purple and blue, with splotches of yellow pulsing here and there.

And then I hear it: the dream of water and sadness. Like a child waiting to catch a dragonfly, I'm afraid to move, afraid the music will stop if I move.

A musical genius, Arias had told us, and the phrase didn't mean anything to me.

Well, now I know what that is: someone who can turn sorrow into sound.

When it is over, I lift my head from my hands. She is holding the guitar to her chest, and her head is tilted to one side. She is looking at me; not looking through me to the wall behind. And I think, for the first time, that she can see me.

THE MOMENT I come through the door, Cecille knows not to nag me about my getting home late again. Maybe she sees something in the sag of my shoulders, in the look on my face, in the way I slide my feet out of my shoes and head straight for the bedroom without a word. I strip off my shirt and drop it into the hamper, go to the bathroom and wash my face. I reach for the face towel on the towel rack near the sink, eyes shut tight against the water trickling down my face; my fingers find it, as well as Cecille's hand, which has taken it off the rack and brought it closer to me. I press both the towel and her palm to my forehead and stand there without moving for a while.

When I open my eyes, I can see her standing behind me in the mirror, her face filled with worry and concern. It's the same look I've seen on her face when one of the kids is sick, or when I've missed out yet again on a promotion, or when I'm working a tough case but she knows better than to ask for details. I feel like I ought to say something, to explain why I'm feeling so awful, but all I can do is shake my head and say, "I don't understand."

She rubs the back of my neck gently, the way she does when soothing one of the kids. "You will." I turn into the warmth behind me and the hurt falls away.

Hours later, I am lying in the darkness, listening to the house. A house will tell you a lot of things people won't. I can hear my wife's regular breathing as she sleeps beside me in the sweet, quiet peace that follows lovemaking; the drip of the faucet in the bathroom sink; the occasional skitter of lizards playing tag on the wooden ceiling. Since it is a small house, the sounds do not have far to travel, they do not break the air and change and become something else other than Cecille's breathing or a dripping faucet or the skitter of lizards. It is a peaceful house—noisy, bustling, cheerfully disorganized in the daytime, slightly calmer but no less cheerful in the evening. The air remembers our laughter, our bargaining over chores and allowances, our problems with math and chemistry and English, our worries about money, our love and hope.

I think about other houses I've been in, how the sounds change in them, how the air smells and feels. I think about how words, voices, anger, fear, malice, linger in the air of a room. How they cling to the walls, how they alter the character of silence.

I don't understand, I told her.

You will, she said.

I'M STANDING IN the house in La Vista. Alvin has left the keys with the neighbors while he vacations with family outside Manila. Some of the furniture is gone; he has sold off things he probably has no right to sell. Inside, the dull resonances of a large and empty house, its doors and windows closed against the sound of birds, the absence of any hum of electricity. Something heavy hanging in the air, something sour and spiteful and unhappy.

I head for the closet—Isa's bedroom, which no one can

ever convince me is habitable. When I open the door, I catch a whiff of ammonia almost immediately; the room has been closed for weeks. I remember the tang of urine in this dark, cramped room, how strong it was when Galvez and I came to pick her up. Galvez had said—I close my eyes and try to remember—he'd said, "Somebody didn't make it to the bathroom in time."

When Galvez walked her out ahead of me, her dress was dry, unstained.

Somebody didn't make it to the bathroom in time.

Who?

The smell wasn't coming from her. It was already in the room.

I turn the bedcovers down. No stains. I look into corners, under the bed, at the piles of folded clothes that lay on the floor, on sheets of newspaper; it occurs to me that she was put in a room with no closets. No closets; no tables; her books and things lying on the floor, lined up against the wall near the door. I walk on my knees to them, geometry and algebra textbooks, notebooks from when she still went to school, dictionaries, Shakespeare and Louisa May Alcott, Nancy Drew mysteries and Archie comics.

As I move, the ammonia scent gets stronger. Men's rooms always smell different from ladies' rooms. Not just different. Worse. Is it because men don't always aim straight? Is it because they don't bother to clean up after themselves? I pass my hands over the tops of the books and boxes and envelopes, exams and class pictures and photo albums, loyalty awards and work ed projects with feathers and yarn.

The tips of my fingers now find edges of paper curled stiff, as though from water damage. My hands stop here.

AS ALWAYS, SHE doesn't react when I come in. I lock the door of the visiting room behind me and go to her. I take her by the elbow—a little more urgently, more roughly than I realize—and make her sit at the table with the music scribbled on it.

I spread the yellowed music books and scores on the table in front of her and wait for a reaction. She glances down at them, then away. Finally, it's her hands that betray her; they open, fingers seeking the paper slowly at first, then with increasing eagerness.

"Did he piss on them?"

She does not react; I forget that she can't hear me. I put out my hand and tilt her chin up so she can read my lips. "Did he piss on them? Was that what made you angry?" She tries to turn away but my fingers grip her chin firmly. "It was okay if you couldn't hear, wasn't it? You didn't need to hear the music to make it. It was in your head. That's why you were brave enough to make yourself deaf. You needed to shut her out to hear the music in your head. Look at me so you can read what I'm saying. He came in that night and pissed on your music. It might not have been the first time, but it was the last. And it was the last straw. You needed to see the music, you needed to be able to read it." I push the books and scores toward her. "You can't read any of these, can you? They're ruined. The ink has run; the pages have gummed together. The photocopies are the worst; you can't salvage any of them. Bach, Vivaldi—all these names I can't pronounce, they all meant something to you. But all of them, lost."

In one swift move she pulls away, shoving her chair back so violently that it falls to the floor. She runs into a corner of the room, crouches low, as though by making herself smaller she will succeed in becoming invisible to me altogether. She presses the palms of her hands to her ears. I follow her; she cringes as I take her by the wrists and pull her hands away from her ears.

"You're deaf, remember? You don't have to do that anymore. You can't hear anything. You can't hear people screaming at you, calling you names. You took care of that. But you couldn't take care of the books. And she didn't stop him—she didn't care. Look at me."

She cries out, a word I can't understand, a non-word, and her voice is hoarse from disuse. It seems to go on a long time. Then words come, one after another, clumping together like candy that has been stored too long in a jar. "*He came in he told me to do the dishes. He said I was too slow he said he would teach me a lesson. I tried to stop him I begged he pissed on them.*" And then she cries out again.

The wailing sounds like a hurt animal in this small, closed room.

I think about my children. I think about how they will probably never get to Disneyland, never play an instrument, never live in a nice big house. I think about my noisy, rowdy, average kids and thank God none of them will ever want to take a pencil and make themselves deaf because that is the only way they can survive. I swear for as long as I live no one will ever, ever piss on the things that are most precious to them, and I take this girl, who is not my child, take her in my arms and hold her. I hold her hoping it will make up for the moment when she told her stepmother about the ruined books and was told to shut up because she deserved it anyway, to go back to that miserable broom closet of a bedroom because she didn't belong upstairs—upstairs in her father's house, in her own house. Hold her for the blinding anger and humiliation and hurt that followed, too much to turn toward herself again. For the horror that came when she realized what she had done. Hold her for her father and mother, who both died not knowing she would come to this, to this moment in this room, with a stranger who knows she has had to do the unthinkable to stay alive.

When the wailing stops, I release her, get up and move to the table. I gather up the books and papers, cross over to the other side of the room and pick up the metal trashcan, and bring them to the corner where she is still crouching. I set the trashcan down between us, show her the books and reach out to take her chin in my hand. "Look at me. *Look at me.* Mr. Arias has copies of these, right?"

She nods.

I stuff the ruined books and scores into the trash. "And you can't use these anymore. Right? So I'm taking them with me."

She nods again.

Later in the day, I fish out the lighter from my pocket and apply the flame to a corner of one of these sheets. The paper catches fire, blackens, the hungry flame moving quickly to the other sheets. I watch the black smoke billow from the trashcan and wait until every scrap of paper is consumed.

SAENZ DROPS BY some days after Isa is released to the custody of a paternal aunt. He sits across me at the desk, hands folded over his chest, and waits for me to start talking about it, the way priests do. For a long time, I say nothing; we stare—me at the ceiling, him at me. The silence between us is filled with understanding.

"I guess she'll be okay now."

"I guess."

"You know, I really didn't have a case."

"Of course not," he says, and for a moment I wonder if he suspects anything. *Impossible*, I tell myself, though I know that's not entirely true. Before I can answer him, he stands and gets ready to leave. But he pats himself down, looking for something, and finally finds it in the square pocket of his shirt. Something small and flat, in a blue plastic bag. He puts it on the desk and slides it toward me.

"What's that?"

"A quick education. For when she starts performing professionally." And he's gone.

I take the package out of the blue plastic bag. It's a cassette tape. *The Instruments of Classical Music: The Guitar and the Lute. Vivaldi. Bach. Rodrigo. Sor. Falla. Dowland.* Strange, unfamiliar names.

I turn it over. With a red felt-tip pen, Saenz has circled one of the selections: no. 4, Bach's Allemande from the Suite in E Minor. I pop the tape into the cassette player, put my feet up on the desk and listen.

DOOR 59

Ten minutes past midnight. The wife hasn't come home yet; Angus's wife, Lila, of the exotic-dancer looks and the weird friends. She parties hard and often forgets Angus in his wheelchair, needing food, needing to go to the bathroom. I saw him when I left the building this morning, just a glimpse of him looking out his window, his thin face full of pain. I don't think he saw me.

Twenty past twelve. I'm afraid I'll fall asleep reading this book: John Pick, *The Arts in a State*. I need to write a paper on it within the next few weeks, something about funding for the arts in the UK. Angus is British; when I was new in the building, house-sitting for my brother and his wife, a neighbor took me to one of the loud parties he and Lila are always throwing. I went just to be polite. Parties don't agree with me, and this was shaping up to be a pretty wild one—thirty people packed in the living room, pounding disco music, bodies dancing too close. As always, I sought the quietest corner, but Angus was there, too. He was in his wheelchair, beer in hand, his eyes alive and the rest of him dead. He's about forty; if he could stand, he would be an inch or two shy of six feet. He has fine, straight hair, a face all sharp planes and angles. I'd started to move away, conscious of intruding into someone else's space. But he spoke: "You want a beer?"

"No, thanks, I don't drink."

"Boy, are you in the wrong place." He took a swig from his bottle. "So do you work in Lila's club?" The Fringe Benefit is a dance club, noisy and smoky and very in with the young, moneyed, and brain-dead, or so my students tell me. Angus put his money in it years ago, along with one or two other night spots and restaurants. Lila runs it now that he can't.

"No. I'm in Door forty-eight."

"Yeah, I thought so. You don't look like any of Lila's friends." He smiled, but the smile stopped at the corners of his mouth; his eyes went dull. "It's okay, then, normal people can't be expected to put up with this." And then he seemed to have forgotten about me. Dismissed, I slunk away, out into the hall and back into the blessed silence of my apartment.

TWELVE-THIRTY. I WONDER if she's coming home at all tonight; sometimes she doesn't. I put down John Pick and walk out of the apartment. Door 59 is one short flight of stairs away. That's how I know Lila isn't home yet; I can always hear the clack of her heels on the marble stairs, and some nights she comes home roaring drunk with a bunch of roaring drunk friends. Well, then, up the stairs I go. At the landing, I stop: Am I making a fool of myself? Worse still, will he think I'm making a fool of him? *You don't think I can take care of myself? You think because I'm in this chair I can't make it to the loo?*

Ah, shut up.

I knock on the door. No answer. Maybe he's asleep. Half a minute and I knock again. Okay. He's definitely asleep. I've been rescued from another act of kindness, or is it conceit? I turn and start down the stairs when I hear his wheels on the wooden floor. His voice sounds feeble from the other side of the door.

"Who is it?"

"It's me. From forty-eight."

He stops to consider this; maybe he's trying to remember if he knows me. "Yes?"

What to say? "I just wanted to know if you're okay."

Another pause, then without conviction: "I'm fine."

"Well, okay. It's just that I noticed Lila isn't home yet."

I hear a sound that could either be a sob or a word that he has smothered in his throat. "Lila isn't home yet," the voice repeats.

"So I was wondering if you needed anything. Do you?" The sound of the wheels as he comes closer to the door, but he does not answer. "Hey. Are you all right?"

He clears his throat as though his last few efforts to speak have tired him. "I'm going to unlock the door, but don't come in until I count to ten. Okay?"

"Sure." I hear the door locks, and the barrel bolt sliding back, and his voice one two three four as the wheels move farther and farther away from the door eight nine ten: okay.

I open the door. He is about ten feet away from me. He is dressed in blue-and-white-striped pajamas, with a red terrycloth towel across his lap. His hair looks greasy. There are circles under his eyes, dark under the pale skin, hollows under his cheekbones and several days' worth of stubble on his face.

I didn't really see the room the last time. Like my apartment, this one has two bedrooms, two bathrooms, a combination living and dining room, a kitchen. Unlike my apartment, this one looks like something out of *Architectural Digest*. The floors are all done in pale wood, the fabrics in white and cream, frosted glass lighting fixtures. On tables and shelves, a fluted Lalique crystal vase, antique plates, an expensive sound system, a freestanding CD rack. Under a glass case, a reproduction, in cream-colored marble, of a detail from an Etruscan frieze: grim-faced, fully armored soldiers and their fierce-looking horses, teeth bared over their bridles, nostrils flaring. I'd been admiring it at the Metropolitan Museum of Art New York shop at Rustan's Shangri-La for months, with an ice cube's chance in hell of being able to buy it. And in one corner, a child-size yellow and lavender tricycle with a basket on the handlebars, incongruous in all this minimalist sophistication, as though it had been left behind by the apartment's previous tenants and overlooked by its present ones.

I take it all in and then look back at him quickly: his eyes, sharp, dark, hooded, are assessing me just as I've assessed his home. "Is there anything I can do for you?" I come closer.

The action provokes an alarming reaction: his hands on the wheels in a flash, spinning wildly, quickly backward.

"No," he cries, "stay where you are." The shrillness of his voice is unnerving.

"Hey, I'm not going to hurt you." I hold out both hands, see, I'm harmless, but the wheels keep turning backward.

"No, don't come any closer."

I'm standing now in the path he has just cut across the living room and I can smell urine and excrement. He sees that I can smell it—some micro-expression on my face has probably given it away—and he puts his hands up before his face, the palms out toward me as though begging not to be hurt. He asks me again not to come any closer.

"Listen, let me help you."

"I don't need any help."

I move forward, crossing the room in long strides to stand at the back of the wheelchair. "Nonsense, I'm a doctor, I'm used to this sort of thing." I wheel him through the bedroom, into the bathroom. Maybe if I act like I know what I'm doing, he'll relax.

The bathroom is just like mine, except they've done wonders with it: the plain white ceramic tiling has been replaced with marble, the sink incorporated into waist-high drawers and cabinets of pale wood. I run a warm bath for him. It takes a while, and the only sounds in the room are the sloshing of the water in the tub and his low, quiet sobbing.

When the tub is half-full, I turn to him. "Ready?" He nods. The pajama top comes off. I slip my forearms under his arms and lift him out of the seat. "Can you hang on?" He nods, and I prop him up; he plants his hands, palms down, onto the flat area around the sink, and manages to remain standing, his weight borne, not by his legs, but by his shoulders and arms. I push the chair away, then peel off his stained pajama bottoms. His adult diapers are soaked through. When I flick the tabs open, the whole thing falls away, heavy with urine and excrement. I have to scrub the caked dirt off before I lower him into the tub. *Okay, get to work, get to work. It's too late to back out now.*

I try not to think about what I'm doing. John Pick's critique of British arts policies. The various forms of licensing in the arts: licensing the audience, licensing the artist, licensing the venue. Regional arts boards and their role in local tourism. Mindlessly scrubbing, scrubbing, and then I hear it: he's sucking air in through his teeth.

"You okay?"

Again that sound, as though he is strangling something he wants to say. "Sores," he finally says. I look at his bottom: the soap and water have cleared away the dirt to reveal small sores, not too serious yet, but they will be in time if they aren't properly cleaned and tended to. "Sorry," I mumble, and then it's back to John Pick, the Royal Charter creating the Arts Council, education as a marketing tool for the subsidized arts.

He's about six or seven inches taller than me, narrow-hipped, wide across the shoulders and back, but shrunken, as though he has lost a lot of weight too fast. With great difficulty, I half drag, half carry him to the tub. He smells, too, of old sweat, and his breath is stale. Lila isn't doing a very good job of taking care of him, but I'm not going to say anything; that's plenty obvious to both of us. The water is warm, warm up to my elbows as I try to make him comfortable in it. I stand up and reach for the soap in its hollow in the wall: not in a million years am I going to be able to buy this kind of soap on a regular basis. *Lather and rub, lather and scrub.* When I look back at him, he is crying quietly into the water, moving his hands and fingers through it as though he has never seen soapy water before. Ribs just under the skin of his torso. I scrub and scrub, and the suds come off him slightly gray. She's doing a lousy job, for my money.

I look around and find the shampoo: great stuff, five hundred pesos a pop for a small bottle, so it says on the bottom. He hums, or moans, or something halfway in between as I wash his hair; slowly, he picks up speed and volume and starts to howl. The sound bounces off the walls and repeats itself, concentric circles on a pool of pain. Don't think, don't judge. Just get on with it. Something throbs inside my head. I wish he would be quiet.

I get up twice, first to grab a toothbrush and some toothpaste, and then a razor and shaving cream. When the shaving is done, I rinse him off. "Towels?" I ask. He points to the full-length mirrors behind me; I look for handles, and they open to reveal a floor-to-ceiling closet with color-coordinated towels, terrycloth robes, bed linen. I choose a white towel and a large white bathrobe, shake them both out, dry him off. "Arms in the holes?" I say, and he nods, slipping his arms through the sleeves of the robe. Another struggle to get him out of the tub, his feet slipping on the slick surface, legs that won't bear him. "Wait here."

He sits on the edge of the tub; I can't let him get back into the wheelchair until I clean that up as well. Soap and water, disinfectant, the works. Scrub until you can't smell anything, nothing but the freshness of Lysol Pine Scent. My arms are starting to hurt but what the hell. *Scrub. Scrub-a-dub-dub.*

"You're good at this."

I almost jump at the sound of his voice, so lost am I in the motions of my scrubbing. "Huh?" I blink stupidly at him.

"I said"—he clears his throat—"I said you're good at this."

In that case I must be a natural at it because you're my first project. "It's a no-brainer."

"I mean, you're good at hiding your feelings. Disgust, for example." It takes him a long time to finish saying it.

Oh, this is a tricky one. Say no and you'll be lying, say nothing and you'll admit it.

"Everybody craps."

"But not in their pants." The laughter in his voice is brittle, forced.

"Well, technically, you were wearing pajamas." I'm done; I get up and wash my hands in the sink, start putting away the sponges and things.

He laughs weakly, but there is no bitterness this time around. "You *are* good at this."

"We aim to please." I stand in front of him and hold my arms out. "Ready?" He reaches up and puts his arms around my neck, and I lift, lift with all my might, drag him to the wheelchair and set him in it as gently as I can. I wheel him out into the bedroom. I didn't get a chance to look at it before, but it's beautiful: the same pale woods, everything white or cream, the expensive linens. I think of my bomb-shelter digs downstairs and grimace; it was a halfway decent apartment when my brother and his wife left, but I've gradually disimproved it over the last seven months. "Pajamas?" He points to a handsome wooden chest of drawers on the other side of the room. "Here? Which one? This one? Right."

On the side of the bed is a three-tiered stainless-steel trolley stocked with medicine, syringes, cotton, alcohol; it's the only thing that looks out of place in this room. At the bottom level of the trolley is a pack of adult diapers, large. I take one; it's a miracle I figure it out as fast as I do. "Okay, here we go." The pajamas come next, and it's over sooner than I think. He smells good. As he arranges his feet and clothes and hands, I take a long look at him: he looks like a different person. Handsome, too, now that he doesn't look so gray, his dark, wet hair like a sleek wing on his head. His face is too thin, though, and his wrists are bony. I turn away just as he looks up at me, and I see the sheets need changing. Right. This shouldn't take long.

When I'm finished, there is a pile of dirty linen on the floor, and I gather it up and put it in the hamper in the bathroom. I come out and he is sitting quietly, hands in his lap. "Okay?" He nods, and again I stand in front of him with my arms out. "Here we go. One-two-three," and I lift. He squirms a little, adjusting himself on the bed, and I put his feet up and under the covers. The building's air conditioning is centralized, and it's always too cold. There's an empty glass on the trolley; I take it and refill it from the sink in the bathroom, come out and set it back in the same place.

I rub my hands together. "So, are you comfortable? Will you be needing anything else?"

He smooths down his pajama shirt. It's likely been days since he wore anything clean. His long fingernails are rimmed with black dirt, and I make a mental note to clean and trim them next chance I get.

"You're in forty-eight."

"Yes."

"Funny I've never seen you before."

"You have. There was this party a while back."

His eyes go dead for a moment. "Lots of parties here." His voice is flat when he says it.

I don't know what to say. "Well, okay. If you need anything, just holler." I head for the door.

"Say, what kind of doctor are you?" he calls from the bedroom as I'm halfway out the door.

"*Of philosophy.*"

I HEARD HER last night, or was it this morning, loud and drunk, her heels on the stairs. I must have stayed awake reading until half past three. Now it's 11 A.M., a Saturday. I don't have to go to school until 2 P.M. I drag myself out of bed and wonder if last night was all just a dream.

I decide to buy a newspaper from the corner store. When I step out into the corridor, she sails past me to the elevator, long black hair and long red nails and legs up to her armpits, a skirt so short another woman might have handily used it for a belt. She casts a backward glance at me, smiles a dazzling smile with two rows of small, perfect white teeth, and then she is gone, leaving a cloud of heavy perfume behind.

I look at their closed door; I wonder if Angus is asleep. I wonder if she asked questions, how did you get cleaned up, how did you manage to change the sheets? Instead of heading down the stairs for my newspaper, I head up to 59.

"Angus?" No sound. "Are you awake?"

He clears his throat. "That you?"

"Yes. How are you doing?"

The wheels on the floor now, and the door opens. He's still in his pajamas; he looks rested. "I'm okay. You going to work?"

"Not till later." I realize I'm still holding on to my milk. "Well, I just wanted to see if you were okay."

"Stay, stay." He wheels himself backward. "I was just going to fix myself some breakfast."

I step inside. The place looks even better in the daylight. "You've done a nice job here."

"Before we were married." He has disappeared into the kitchen. "I was still working then. Money to burn." I hear utensils and plates, take my time looking at the treasures in the living room before following him. Everything in the kitchen is first-rate as well: a large four-burner stove, a stainless-steel hood, a fancy dishwasher. A cast-iron pot rack hangs above a square wooden table in the center and from it, copper-bottomed pots and pans. The china and pantry cabinets are made of pale burled wood with glass doors. "You cook?"

"I used to." The kitchen was not built for a wheelchair-bound person; everything is too high, and there is nothing for him to hold on to. The top of the kitchen island comes up to his chest and he has to lift his arms to the level of his shoulders to reach it. There's half a loaf of old, dry-looking French bread in front of him, two plates, two glasses of water; for a few seconds the room is silent save for the rasp of the serrated knife as he slices the hard bread with infinite patience. I look at him. Something passes from my mind to my face and he catches it before I can catch myself, puts the knife down on the table. That sound he makes in his throat; I don't know his wife all that well, but right now, hearing it, I could very happily kill her.

"Why don't I whip up something for us?" I stupidly blunder, opening the sleek black refrigerator, sticking my head in and finding—nothing? Nothing but water and white wine?

Again that sound, Jesus Christ, as though he is choking on an apology for being alive.

"Lila isn't much of a cook," he says slowly when he finds the words. *No, she isn't much of anything, is she?* But I stop myself from saying it. The effort of not saying it shows on my face when I take it out of the refrigerator.

"Wait here," I say, as though he had a choice. I run out of the apartment and down to my flat, into my kitchen. I grab a wire basket and fling the door of my fridge open:

eggs, ham, butter, onions, vegetables, soft white bread, and my favorite grape jam, the only true luxury in my life apart from high-quality photocopying of library books. Everything goes into the basket and then I'm bounding up the stairs again, into Door 59 and its beautiful, empty kitchen. I start ransacking the place for bowls and spoons and forks and plates and pans and salt and pepper. There's a toaster in the corner and I grab it as well.

"What are you making?" He wheels himself toward me as I flick on one of the gas burners.

"A frittata. Like an omelet, only better." I'm lecturing a man who probably knows more about cooking than I do, if his kitchen is anything to go by. Butter in the pan, sauté the vegetables and the ham, pour in the beaten eggs, wait for them to set then flip the whole thing over so the runny part lands on the bottom. A minute or two more over the burner, then turn it out onto a plate. The toast is ready, everything on the table now. He looks and looks, spoon in one hand, fork in the other. "Go on," I say.

He starts out slow, a bite of buttered toast here, some of the frittata. I guess I expect him to speed up, but he doesn't: he maintains this perfectly polite pace, chewing well, spooning food into his mouth slowly. He finishes a fourth of the omelet, two pieces of toast, and then he lays down the spoon and the fork on the side of the plate and smiles a small smile of contentment.

"Would you save the rest for me?"

"You can have as much as you want now, and then I can make you something else for later."

And then it happens, the hunger asserting itself over the demands of politeness and refinement. He takes up his spoon and fork, and then he picks up speed, faster and faster, utensils stabbing into the mouth again and again, and then abandoned in favor of fingers, grabbing greasy fistfuls of egg and buttered toast, and then the tears again, running down his face and salting his food, food down his chin, down the front of his pajamas, his mouth full as he begins again like last night, that same terrible howling.

I'M A PRETTY solitary person; most of the time I feel removed from people and things, standing on the outside and pressing my nose to the window of life, neither daring nor caring to walk in. I don't know why I do it, and I don't want to dig deeper to find out. All our motives are suspect; somebody once said there's no such thing as altruism. Be that as it may, Angus is my project. Every morning before I go to school, I make him some breakfast and maybe a sandwich for lunch if I'm really in a hurry. I change his diapers and put him in jeans and a shirt. I've learned to give him his painkillers: with a syringe, even though I hate needles. I practiced for an hour on a slab of pork belly so there would be no surprises.

I used to dawdle at my faculty office well into the evening, postponing as long as possible having to face the safe, snug emptiness of the apartment. Now I rush home as soon as I can, and my friends ask me the usual questions about having "someone in my life." *Well, yeah, I guess you could say that, but not quite in the way you mean.*

When I get home—around 7 P.M. if the traffic is bad—I go straight to Door 59 with my books and my papers to change him, then back downstairs to fix us dinner. A couple of weeks ago I bought some cookbooks; I'd already exhausted my limited repertoire of sandwiches and soups and omelets. It isn't as though she starves him, he argues; she just forgets what's in the fridge. Right.

After dinner we listen to his CDs or watch movies; he has a huge collection of great ones on DVD and Blu Ray: Eisenstein's *Battleship Potemkin*, *The Rules of the Game*, *Nosferatu*. Garbo in *Ninotchka*, Dietrich in *The Blue Angel*, Simone Signoret in *Room at the Top*. I practice my phrasebook French on him—he speaks the language fluently—and he sniggers unhelpfully when I ask some imaginary waiter for *la carte des vins, s'il vous plait*, or some invisible French matron, *Cela ne vous ennuie pas que je fume?* Both completely pointless to learn since I neither drink nor smoke.

When it's time to turn in, or when I have to go downstairs to work, I give him a bath and change him back into pajamas. On weekends I do his laundry. He doesn't howl anymore.

I try not to be around when Lila is there; I don't know if my presence will precipitate more cruelty, more neglect. Some days I think of confronting her: Hello? That's your husband in there? Do you think you could come home before midnight once in a while? Change his sheets and his diapers more often? Feed him, for God's sake?

And other days I want to ask him why he doesn't just get rid of her. Are you broke? Sell off some of your stuff, and

I'll find you some work you can do from a wheelchair. Usually though I just shut up. There must be a reason he lives this way, must be a reason why he puts up with this. There's a part of me that actually wants to believe this. Maybe he really loves her. Maybe it's none of my damn business, even if I have taken over most of the duties a loving wife should be performing for a disabled husband.

For thirty-four years I've built a quiet little four-cornered life: my job, my books, my computer, the occasional brush with my family. Angus has traveled the world and lived the way most people only dream about living. He grew up in Scotland, in a small village overlooking the Tay. And yes, he can play the bagpipes if you beg pretty, please. He spent summers in Malta and Greece, moved to England with his family at twelve, got a degree from the London School of Economics. His memories play like those beautifully filmed documentaries on the BBC or the Discovery Channel: biking through Provence, the perfect calm of a sunset in the Grand Canyon, swimming with turtles in the Sargasso Sea. As he talks fondly and without arrogance about a dead life, I can see what an absolute devil he must have been, long before he was this thin and pale, long before the accident and this wheelchair and the prison his body has become.

The yellow bicycle belonged to Lila's daughter, Maggie. Lila was the black sheep in a good family. Pregnant at sixteen, she dropped out of college after having the baby, drank, did drugs. Several run-ins with the law, though her parents and their money made it all disappear. She partied with her friends at bars and dance clubs like the Fringe Benefit. That's where she met Angus, white, educated, well-off.

Her family had been wary at first—*dear Lord, not another one of these Eurotrash types she's always hanging out with.* But then he seemed to be good for her. She reined in the drinking, got off the drugs. He put her to work at the club, front of the house, then found she had a surprisingly good head for business. She and Maggie moved in with him and they all seemed happy for a while. She'd stumbled on a chance to finally turn her life around.

Then Maggie started getting sick a lot, and nobody knew exactly from what. They seemed to spend a lot of time in hospitals. Angus was taking her in his car to yet another hospital when the accident happened: a bus ran them off the road near the treacherous Boni Avenue overpass. Maggie died instantly; Angus's spine broke in several places and his pelvis was shattered.

He takes nothing for granted: everything I do, no matter how small, is worth a *thank you*. For me, this is all pretty heady stuff, being needed, being appreciated—cocaine for a bleeding heart.

Every once in a while, though, I say something stupid, intrude on some past hell whose doors he wants to keep closed. One night I'm putting away a couple of CDs we've listened to when it occurs to me there are no happy-family pictures of Angus and Lila and Maggie anywhere in the apartment: only photos of Angus with friends, a couple of shots from his many travels.

"Hey, Angus," I call out to him from the living room, "don't you have any pictures of the three of you together?"

I know immediately it wasn't a good question to ask. Though I know he heard me, it's a while before he comes out of the kitchen, and he doesn't speak at once when he does. "We put those away," he says quietly.

"And Lila is okay with that?"

"Things are different now." His face is expressionless, as though he is far away. Then, without another word, he rolls himself back into the kitchen. I don't ask any more questions.

I'VE HAD A few bad days in Door 59, but this day by far is the worst. I go up early—around 7 A.M.—with Angus's breakfast on a plate. I'm already dressed for work because I've got a faculty meeting at eight. I knock on the door and Angus opens it immediately. "Ssshh," he says, putting a forefinger to his lips. He wheels himself out of my way and motions for me to follow him into the kitchen.

"Lila had another hard day's night?" I whisper with a smirk. He nods without smiling; I put the plate of food on the table, and he seems uneasy, eager to get rid of me. "I'm going, I'm going. Will you be okay?"

Suddenly a man appears at the door of the kitchen; shirtless, he is wearing one of Angus's pajama bottoms, which are so long on him that the hems bunch up at his ankles. He is about twenty-six. He has good muscle tone and a blue tattoo on one arm, the head of a woman giving a disembodied man a blow job and the words ORGAN DONOR beneath.

Long hair down to his shoulders, vacant eyes. He scratches his tummy as he yawns. "Got any coffee here?"

Angus sits perfectly still; for a split second I wonder if he's died, and then he raises a hand and points to one of the pantry cabinets. "Bottom shelf," he says, his face expressionless, and then he hustles me out of the kitchen toward the front door. On our way out, I hear Lila call out sleepily from the bedroom: "Black. No sugar." I stop in the middle of the living room, staring in the direction of her voice, until I feel Angus's knees in the wheelchair bumping hard against my legs, pushing me forward. I step out of the door and wait, giving Angus a hard stare. He doesn't look at me.

"Thanks."

"Angus, where did you sleep last night?"

He takes a deep breath, as though he's too tired to explain. "It's okay. I slept just fine."

"You're not answering my question."

"Thanks for breakfast." He closes the door.

"Angus, will you come out here? Angus? Angus, talk to me."

I stand outside the door for a while. When I go downstairs, my heart is beating a hole in my chest. Damn, damn, damn it all. I get to the sidewalk, and everything seems unreal. I need to get to the bus stop, but my feet won't move except to pace quickly in a tight circle; I can't breathe. "Jesus," I find myself screaming to no one in particular, "Jesus CHRIST." People give me strange looks and cross the street to avoid me.

• • •

WE'RE SITTING IN front of the wide windows in the living room on a perfect Saturday morning and when I look at him, I realize his face is very nearly the same color as his white T-shirt. "How long has it been since you were out there? In the real world?"

"You mean, working?"

"No, I mean just out there. In the sun."

Oh, he says soundlessly, drumming his fingers on the armrest of the wheelchair, frowning, trying to remember. "Couple of years. I think when I came home from the hospital," without a hint of complaint.

The neighbors say he's been wheelchair-bound for the last two years. "Are you under house arrest or something?"

He chuckles, throws up his hands. "No more Olympic competitions for me."

Early the following Saturday, I get Leo from 52 to help me lay some thick plyboard down the stairs and then I knock on Angus's door. He opens it and sees the two of us. "Hey."

"Good, you're up." I wheel him around quickly to the bathroom for his morning ablutions.

"Why, what's going on?"

"We're going out. *Allons nous balader.*"

"What?"

"Hey, that came out rather well." I pretend offense, but the puzzlement does not leave his face and I realize it's not a commentary on my pronunciation. "Out. You know. Sunlight, fresh air, speed bumps. Out."

Leo hangs out in the living room until we're ready. Then

we wheel Angus out and huff and puff our way down the makeshift ramp to the elevator.

In the lobby, the receptionist's eyes widen. She gets out from behind the counter, takes his hand and squeezes it and shakes it hard. He's been kind to her; I can tell from the tears in her eyes. She says she's wanted to come up and see him but was afraid of his wife. He pats her hand and says he understands. She says she wishes he could get a phone up there. He smiles and nods, maybe someday.

Outside, the van I've hired for the day is waiting. The driver folds up the seats in the back and helps Leo and me put Angus in, wheelchair and all.

Leo assures me he'll be around to help when we get back. "I'll be in all day," he says.

We're off. There's lots of places we could go, but today, with the sun not too bright and the weather breezy, I can't think of a better place than the UP Diliman campus. Okay, I'm cheap. But today's thrills aren't. There's an open-air concert at the Sunken Garden, the UP Guitar Ensemble playing a Brandenburg concerto, among other things. I packed some lunch. I want him to see some trees.

The ensemble does not disappoint. Angus holds the basket with our lunch in his lap, taps his knee with a forefinger in time with the music; at one point, I see him crying into his hands. I look away quickly, search the crowd for anybody else who might be looking at him; satisfied that nobody else is, I realize with some astonishment how protective I feel over him. The astonishment holds a mild undercurrent of uneasiness; if I feel this strongly after only three months, how will I feel after six? After twelve?

The concert ends at eleven. I wheel him around the academic oval, slowly, so he can take it all in: the grass, the trees, the air, the athletes kicking a soccer ball around on one side of the field, the students coming out of their Saturday classes in groups, life. Neither of us talks.

Under one of the big spreading trees across the BA building, I take the basket from him and lay out a small blanket, spread it on the grass and help him out of the wheelchair to sit on it, legs stretched out over its blue-and-red stripes. The sun is high now, but so is the wind. Down on the field, a couple of children are flying a red kite with a long red tail; they let out more and more string until I can barely see the spot of red against the brilliant blue sky. But the kite doesn't interest Angus; he looks at the children, hungrily it seems, as though he'll never see another one again. He senses me looking at him and he turns to me, waiting.

"Kids," I say, not very helpfully.

"Goddamn miracle, every last one." He shuts his eyes tight against an image or images that he's already remembering against his will, like a little old lady locking the front door while a burglar rummages blithely through her underwear drawers.

"Angus, you have to get out." He doesn't respond, just turns his head away, the wind lifting a lock of hair off his forehead. "Angus? You hear me?" He nods. "You don't have to live like this. Cooped up in that apartment for years, no phone, no medical attention, no contact with the outside world."

"I get medical attention."

"From her?" I can't keep from smirking. "A handful of painkillers every day does not constitute medical attention. You ought to be doing physical therapy. You might still be able to get out of that chair."

He finally opens his eyes, turns and smiles at me. "You're a good kid."

"Why do you put up with it?"

He lies back on the grass and crosses his arms over his forehead. "You must read a lot."

"Sure. Comes with the job."

"You've read Poe, right? Edgar Allan Poe? Lot of people think he wrote proto-pulp, but I like him all the same."

He pauses. "'The Telltale Heart.' You remember that? Guy kills somebody, the authorities come to ask him a couple of questions, he keeps hearing the victim's heart beating under the floorboards. *Pom-PUMP, pom-PUMP.*" He puffs his cheeks up and expels the air with every second syllable. "Goes crazy, turns himself in just so he can get away from it."

He seems elsewhere now, lost in thought. "Everybody's got a heart beating under the floorboards. Everybody."

WHEN WE GET back to the apartment, Leo is waiting outside the building; I see his worried face as our van pulls up. I get out and he comes up to me. "She's back. And she's not happy."

"She can go to hell." I walk around to the back to wait for the driver. I take Leo's arm. "Don't tell him anything. I'll take care of it."

The three of us help bring Angus out of the back and into the building. We go up in the elevator; Leo has laid the plyboard back on the stairs. As we wheel him up the ramp to their apartment, the door opens, and Lila emerges. Her mouth is a red slash, hands balled into fists on either side of her waist, her eyes flashing. "Well. You've been busy. Did you enjoy yourselves?"

"Lighten up," I say; from the corner of one eye, I see Leo struggling with the plyboard and scurrying away.

"I'm not talking to you." She turns to Angus. "You're not supposed to leave the apartment."

"It was just one morning, Lila." He sounds like a child caught playing hooky, trying to weasel his way out of being grounded or spanked. It makes me furious.

"Get inside. I'll deal with you later." Angus wheels himself inside the apartment, and she closes the door behind him and stands in front of it, facing me with her arms crossed over her chest. "So. You're the Good Samaritan."

"There are laws to protect your husband from the things you do to him." I turn and head back down the stairs. She comes after me, catching up at my door.

"Aren't you the smart one?" She comes closer, circling me. "Some kind of teacher, right?" Her head tilts to one side and her eyes narrow, as though I am a curious animal she's never seen before. "What do you know about us? What has he told you?"

I unlock the door. "He doesn't need to tell me anything. I have eyes."

"Do you?" She places herself in the open doorway, then slides into my apartment without hesitation. "Good. Then you've noticed that he doesn't keep any of our photographs."

I snort in disgust. "I wouldn't keep photos of you either." It's the mother of all lame comebacks, and she and I both know it. She laughs and laughs, a high-pitched neigh that grates on the ear, and all the while she's laughing, she's going around my living room touching my things, my books, my pillows, my family pictures on a bookcase. I don't want her here, I don't want her perfume in my living room, I don't want her hands on my stuff. "Please leave."

"Oh, aren't I as welcome in your home as you are in ours?" She flops down on my sofa, crosses her long legs, hugs a throw pillow to her chest.

"Get out."

"Why don't you ask him about Maggie? Does he ever talk to you about her?"

"She died in an accident. Now please get out."

The laugh again. "And I'm sure everyone told you he was taking her to the hospital for a checkup." She stops laughing, and suddenly her face looks old, old and tired and sad under the makeup. "My daughter was a beautiful child. I couldn't tell you how beautiful, how happy and bright she was. A few months after Angus and I got married, she started getting sick. Losing weight, throwing up, having nightmares. She became withdrawn and moody. I couldn't figure out what was wrong with her."

"Listen, I don't want to hear any of this."

"But you must. After all, you're a part of our lives now." She hugs the pillow tighter. "One day I ask him to take her to the doctor for one of her checkups because I'm anxious to finish the monthly accounts for the club. After he leaves, an email pops up in the club's inbox. I don't recognize the sender's name, it's not anyone I know. There's no subject, no message. Just an attachment. But the file name is 'Maggie.'"

"They must have missent it to the club's email address. So I open it. And it's a video, set to music." As she tells me the story, I begin to realize she's not here at this moment. She's in that room, sitting in front of that computer, watching something horrific unfold on the screen. "And then it all makes sense. The mood swings. The nightmares."

"I can't think straight. I grab the phone and call him. I'm screaming. I tell him I'll call the police and have him arrested. At first, he tries to deny it, tells me to calm down. But when I don't, he says nobody will ever believe me. Me, with my past, with the drinking and the drugs. Says that if I try anything, he'll find a way to keep me quiet." She stands up, takes the pillow, and heaves it at the bookcase. The picture frames topple over. "And then he reminds me that she's right there in the car with him. And that if I say a word to anyone, I'll never see her again. That he'll take her far, far away, someplace I'll never be able to find her."

"Then she started to scream, and that was the last time

I ever heard her voice." Lila's eyes are wet, but she's angry. She's cultivated this anger over the years, nurtured it like she might have done with the child who was no longer there, turned it into a weapon. "She was six when she died, have people told you that? Six years old and all skin and bones. And yet in a way she's better off dead than here with him. You don't have any children, I suppose?"

"No."

She walks toward me, slowly, slowly, leans close until her face is inches from my own.

"Someday you might. And we'll talk again."

She walks out and closes the door behind her. I'm standing completely still, but the room feels as though it has been moved, floor and all.

TEN A.M. ON Sunday. I wake up late; couldn't sleep last night, too many thoughts racing through my head, or maybe just one.

What do you know about us? she'd asked me. But now I have to ask myself: *What do you know about you?*

I wonder if I'll make breakfast for Angus today. He must be hungry by now. He must be wondering what's taking me so long.

THE ONE CRY

Her name was Jessilyn. I remember thinking, when I first heard it, that it was one of those funny made-up names jeepney drivers are forever painting on the interiors of their jeeps: Jessilyn, Janilyn, Jerrilyn, Jennalyn. Often some mishmash of the father's and mother's name, or else an imitation of the name of some popular teenage singer or starlet. Usually one of a string of similar names of siblings in the same family, small people living small lives, in cramped spaces with illegal water and power connections.

Strange how a name can mark you.

This Jessilyn lived in a cramped space with no water and no power connections, with distant relatives, in the town of Posadas, Davao. She died, or so people said at first, on a street that was always brightly lit at night, on the one night in Posadas when everybody was sure to be dressed in their Sunday best and out of their homes and out in the streets: the mayor's birthday. She died just when these same brightly lit streets should have been safest. Her body was found wedged between a sari-sari store and one wall of the town's Methodist church compound, her jeans pulled down to her thighs, her underwear missing. Her broken umbrella, her shoulder bag, her wallet with a crisp five hundred-peso bill in it, all lying in the dirt beside her. Her watch, a Valentino quartz that probably cost just a little over two hundred pesos, still on her wrist, still ticking on past that moment when she'd breathed her last.

I ARRIVE IN Posadas two weeks after the murder, still reeling from the bumpy two-hour ride in a packed van from Baticuling, the nearest town. Jessilyn's Manila relatives had begged someone, anyone from the media to listen to them, to come and help. They'd also told me that Posadas was about fifteen minutes away from Baticuling, and that if you were enterprising enough you could walk there. I should have remembered that people from rural areas reckon time and distance differently from the rest of us.

I don't have much time to cover this story—three days, maybe four if I find anything interesting. As far as the news cycle goes, this one's already overripe, and I should have moved on to something else days ago. But there's something in the family's anger, in their fierce persistence, that's drawn me in.

I check into what is probably the best hotel in town, judging from its name: D'Best Hotel and Inn. I am promptly shown into a small room with high louvered windows, wooden floors and hospital-green walls, and a bed with a dull red bedcover. The teenager who brought up my stuff opens the bathroom door for me, and the door falls off one hinge, hanging askew by the two remaining ones. A roach crawls out of the bathroom like a tourist strolling down a sunny beach.

I tip the boy twenty pesos and he closes the door

behind him. The green walls are scrawled over with all the indications that this is a regular hangout for locals who can't scratch an itch in the bedrooms of their own homes: *Jun+Ester, love forever; theres nothing like a woman who love you all nite; call me Lala tel. no. $%#^; Alice is da bes in da wes.* The establishment has decided it's not worth the time or effort or money to paint over all these. The red bedcover is stained in places, even though it reeks of detergent and fabric softener.

I check my watch; I'm meeting the freelance photographer hired by the paper's Davao office at the Posadas police station at nine. Tony Javier and I have worked together several times before. He is a small man, and he looks even smaller beside the five feet seven and one hundred and eighty pounds of me. For two decades, he worked for a foreign press agency, and he was very, very good at what he did, traveling the world photographing floods and famines, earthquakes and election campaigns, wars both brief and protracted, every last one of them dirty and unnecessary. His instincts were sharp, his pictures unforgettable.

But he'd seen too many things he'd wanted to forget and decided to pull the plug before they were all he could remember. He plowed his dollars into a small farm in Davao after the last elections and settled into comfortable semi-retirement. Now, unlike me, he only works when he feels like it.

I put my bags on the utility table by the windows. Across the street, with its doors still closed for the day, is the

D'Licious Nightclub Karaoke Restaurant. No wonder the stains on the bedcover.

I FIND TONY leaning against the doorway of the Posadas police station and community hall. He has none of the usual trappings of the local press photographer-slash-fixer: no paparazzi vest, no layers of laminated IDs, no aviator shades. A small black camera bag and a camera, that's all, and he always shows up in immaculate white shirts (more fashion photographer than press) and clean slacks or jeans cut close to his legs, long for such a short guy.

Certain small men feel compelled to transcend their smallness by being natty dressers; Tony is natty to the point of rakishness, even now that he lives out here in the provinces, where he is often mistaken for some slumming provincial governor. His hair is wavy, longish, thick; he wears a mustache, and he walks the way a very tall man would walk, all rangy, loose-limbed, laid-back cool, the knees never touching. He's not my type, but even I have to admit he's attractive, and all the more so for being concentrated in such a small package.

He does not move to meet me halfway; he waits for me to come up the three or four steps to the entrance, his head tilted to one side and slightly back. In the back of my mind, I realize he has set it up so that within the first few seconds of my seeing him, he will be momentarily taller than I am.

"Joanna." He's never called me Joe, the way everyone I know calls me. He always uses my full name, and he always says it slowly, *Jo-AH-nna*, as though he likes the taste of it in his mouth.

"Tony. Seen the photos?" I hold out a pack of three-by-fives that Jessilyn's Manila relatives gave me before I left. Some are amateur shots of the girl's body, snapped by her own brother with a cheap camera before she was taken away for further examination.

He does not take them; he has obviously seen copies retained by her family here. "Night duty officer's here." He jerks his thumb in the direction of an overweight uniformed man in rubber flip-flops.

I brush past Tony to approach the officer. "Excuse me. Hi. You're Captain Sucgang?"

"Yes, ma'am."

"Elfren Sucgang, right? You received the complaint?"

"Yes, ma'am." His face is slack, the face of a man who does not often tax his mind. He motions for me to take the seat in front of his desk, and he takes his own seat. Underneath the desk, a pair of rubber boots with things stuffed in them—plastic and damp rags. The smell of them wafts up to me, old sweat and mold.

"Okay, can you tell me what happened that night?"

"Ma'am, the suspect came in and confessed to killing Miss Jessilyn Samson." He pauses and looks at me, at my hands, wondering perhaps why I'm not taking down notes. I motion for him to continue. "He told us where he leave the body. We sent two police mans with him and they confirmed that Miss Jessilyn Samson is dead."

"This suspect, that's Elmer Quitorio, right?"

"Yes, ma'am." Even though I'm speaking in Tagalog, he insists on answering me in halting English. "He is in his forties. He is not very healthy in the mind. He is also drunk on the night of the murder."

"I see." I wonder how he would define being healthy in the mind. "Did he say how he killed her?"

"I think ma'am, there is a love triangle." *Okay, here we go.* The love triangle, however farfetched, seems to me the motive of choice to which most provincial police officers attribute violent crime, second only to both political ideology—*he's a Communist*—and drug dealing. "I think ma'am this Elmer was in love with Miss Jessilyn Samson. He said so. He said Miss Jessilyn has another boyfriend and he got jealous. He attempted to take Miss Jessilyn by force and he did forced her to have an intercourse with him."

I steal a glance at Tony standing quietly in one corner, staring hard at his shoes and trying not to laugh. "Okay, how did he kill her?"

"He said ma'am that he hit her some times. Then she lost unconsciousness. He wake her up but she would not."

"Did he do this near the sari-sari store?"

"No, ma'am, inside in the compound. We will bring you."

"Okay, bring me."

TONY FILLS ME in on Elmer as he and I bounce around in the back of the police van. "He recanted about three days later. Said the real killer made him confess to the crime, threatened him and his family if he didn't."

"He's a distant relative of hers, right?"

"Right. She was staying as a boarder in his family's home here in Posadas because it was nearer where she worked than her hometown, Cacdang, where she lived with her parents."

"And she worked in the mayor's cockpit."

"Right. She would stay late at the cockpit about two or three times a week and a service vehicle would drop her off at the street corner near the Methodist church."

"And Elmer would usually wait for her there and accompany her home." I go through the pack of photographs, look at the ones in which Jessilyn Samson was alive and well, happy, a pretty nineteen year old with fair skin and clear eyes, obviously popular in her rather large circle of friends. Here she is in the peaked cap and uniform of a fast-food outlet where she used to work as a cashier; here in a ruffled dress at her high school graduation; here in a majorette's red outfit, twirling a baton in front of a marching band. "Did you manage to get me an appointment with the medico-legal officer?"

"Local health officer," Tony corrects me, my first indication she may not be as qualified as one might hope. "Dr. Perpetua Cabigting. On leave since the fifteenth." He doesn't have to spell it out; it's clear she's not meant to be around while I'm in town.

"This Elmer. His first story is consistent with at least some of the girl's injuries."

Tony shrugs. "But *he* isn't. The girl had a good four or five inches on him, and she was strong. You'll see."

• • •

WE ARRIVE AT the compound where Jessilyn was supposed to have been killed. It's not really a compound, just a huge open lot. There's no entryway, no gate, just the sari-sari store to one side. I pause for a moment near the store, the dirt there dark brown, compact, loamy. Inside are several small homes, some just huts or shacks, others more substantial, with concrete walls and roofs of rusty corrugated metal. In the middle of the lot, a large patch of overgrown brush, a few dying banana trees, a few rows of scraggly corn.

Sucgang and another officer—surly, sour-faced Pineda—pick their way much too carefully through the undergrowth, trying to look like they know what they're doing. Snakes or frogs, they look like they would be happy here, in the moist earth and the thick underbrush. Fearing reptiles, hating amphibians, I crash through, flattening plants without mercy.

We come to a small clearing, past the rows of corn, bounded by a low hollow-block wall. To the left, on the other side of the wall, two or three very small houses; on the right, a makeshift shed that has recently been emptied. Sucgang says Elmer used to make reed baskets and furniture here, small tables, chairs, shelves. This is where he first said he raped the girl, before he recanted.

"Elmer and his sisters live in that one." Sucgang points with his forefinger at one of the houses, low, concrete, with a galvanized-iron roof. "Jessilyn was a boarder there."

"Anybody see or hear anything?"

"The old caretaker at the Methodist church say she

only heard one scream. But she say she didn't think it was important. There were many people out celebrating that night." It occurs to me that Sucgang is convinced of Elmer's guilt, and before long he's trying to convince me as well. "He looks small, ma'am, but he is strong or else he cannot bend the sticks he uses for baskets." *Wiry strength; hey, it's a possibility.*

I turn to Tony and he nods, begins snapping away with his camera. I walk into the shed; the dirt floor is covered with a thick layer of sawdust and wood shavings.

"And this is where he is supposed to have raped her."

"Ma'am, based on his first confession, yes." *The first confession, which you believe, despite the fact that it doesn't make sense. The pictures of the body, her T-shirt pushed up to just underneath her breasts, the jeans pulled down to midthigh. The brother not a professional photographer, but somehow managing to capture on film some details that bug me: the bloodied mouth, the large gray grains of sand and bits of broken shell on her skin, nothing like this sawdusty dirt, certainly nothing like the dark brown soil near the sari-sari store.*

"Where exactly?"

Sucgang points to a patch even thicker with sawdust. I find half-buried in the shavings a pink plastic hairbrush, the kind with rounded bristle tips, cheap, the handle broken off. It's probably not hers, but Tony snaps it anyway.

"So the old caretaker hears one cry all the way from the church premises." I turn toward the small houses on the other side of the hollow-block wall. "And the people in those houses. Did they hear anything?" Sucgang blinks,

Pineda shrugs, and between the two of them I get my answer.

"And why would he bring her all the way to the sari-sari store from here?" Little Elmer carrying tall, unconscious Jessilyn the distance from here to the entrance of the compound, in the dead of night, through the brush. It doesn't add up.

"He said he felt guilty, and he wanted to take her to the hospital." Guilty little Elmer, stopping first to pull the jeans back onto her body, gather up her handbag and her umbrella. The long walk through the darkness, through the darkness and the brush carrying the unconscious Jessilyn. If I were half-wit Elmer, guilty, afraid, what would I have done? Wouldn't I have just run, better to just run, to disappear? Why would I take the trouble of bringing her to a hospital—would I even think of that? Would I remember her bag and her umbrella, would I try to put her clothes back on?

And where would I have put her underwear?

"Did you find her panties?"

"No ma'am." No panties. The bag, the umbrella, the jeans but no panties. Thinking back on the pictures again, the stains down the front of her jeans. Did Elmer just pull them down, rip off the panties and then rape her? And if that was the case, shouldn't the panties just be lying around, would he have taken the trouble to throw them elsewhere?

"When he recanted, what exactly did he say?"

"He said he was sleeping in here since seven P.M. He woke up on eleven thirty. He said he went to fetch Miss

Jessilyn on the usual hour but he found a man putting her near the sari-sari store."

"Could he tell if she was alive?"

"Ma'am I don't know."

"Okay, this man Elmer says he saw, could he identify him?"

"Ma'am, he said it was a certain Erning whom he has seen with Miss Jessilyn before."

"And did you find him?"

"Yes ma'am but he was released. For lack of evidence ma'am."

"Where is he now?"

"I'm sorry ma'am but I don't know."

"You don't know." I take a deep breath. "Okay. Did you get his address and his full name?"

"Ma'am, because there was no evidence."

It's hot here and this man is getting on my nerves. "His full name. His address."

"He lives in Posadas ma'am." Thank you, and so do some three thousand other people, your census takers say.

A random thought: before I left Manila, I was reading some research in the UK on the relationship between victim and criminal—*if the criminal is under twenty-six years of age there is a strong likelihood that he lives within a 2.5 mile radius of his victim's residence, twenty-five miles if he's over twenty-six.* Apparently, the British police can tell with a reasonable degree of certainty if a crime has been committed by a young man. I try to think if this was such a crime. Elmer is not a young man, he is in his mid to late forties. He is not a man who has his wits about him, from what I can tell from the police reports, from his confession, from his recantation, from Sucgang. He does not socialize other than selling the things he makes or buying his daily needs.

The victim is young, popular with young people, moves in young people's circles. So then, is this a young man's crime?

"Officer Sucgang, who was the investigating officer that night?"

Sucgang looks at me as though I have caught him in a lie. "Sergeant Lagunsod ma'am."

"Where can I find him?"

Sucgang swallows, his Adam's apple working up and down just beneath the skin of his throat. "Ma'am he has been transferred ma'am."

"Since when?"

"Ma'am June tenth ma'am."

"Where is he now?"

"Ma'am I do not know."

"You don't? Aren't you supposed to know?"

"Ma'am I do not know."

How convenient. First the health officer that examined the body goes on leave; now we find out that the investigating officer has been reassigned, God knows where.

"Joanna." This must be the third or fourth time Tony has called me; I've been lost in thought.

"Yeah."

"I said let's go see Elmer."

● ● ●

THE PROVINCIAL JAIL is a few run-down buildings with a large open space in the middle, surrounded by high whitewashed walls and a few puny strands of chicken wire. We are shown into a dingy room with a series of increasingly large brown wooden desks—the rule being, the bigger the desk, the more important the occupant. Gray-green filing cabinets are pushed up against the walls, and stale air blows through large electric fans that probably haven't been taken apart and cleaned since they were first bought, their blades thickly furred at the edges with dust and dirt. There are windows on one side of the room, some of them without glass panes. To the frame of one of these windows, someone has chained a small, ill-tempered, dun-colored monkey.

Elmer is brought into the room by several police officers, with much fanfare. Some ice-cold Pepsis and Clubhouse crackers arrive soon after—for our benefit, not his. I look at him. The man has pale pink skin, mottled just under his throat with age spots, hair cropped close to the skull. He is just a little over five feet tall, and yes, he does have a look of wiry strength about him. But the face—there's something about the face, stupid but harmless, the eyes both bewildered and empty. He looks almost astonished to be here, like he just woke up to find himself in a completely different place from where he went to sleep.

The officers make quick introductions in the local dialect. He blinks repeatedly, but it's clear nothing's really sinking in.

"Hey, Elmer." I speak quietly, try not to be my usual

brusque self. "You're being accused of something very serious." He nods sadly. "Why don't you tell me what happened?"

Through a police interpreter, Elmer says he woke up, fearing he had overslept and was late to pick the girl up from the corner and escort her home as usual. He went out by the sari-sari store and found a man—he could only remember the name as Erning—arranging Jessilyn's body in the space between the wall of the Methodist church compound and the sari-sari store.

Erning looks up, sees Elmer, threatens him, punches him in the face, tells him to confess to the crime, *I know where your family lives, I know your sister's pregnant, I can kill all of you, I will kill all of you if you tell anyone what you saw tonight.* Erning rushes off, Elmer attends to the unconscious Jessilyn.

The monkey in the window turns somersaults, then screeches combatively at the people in the room. The officers smirk conspiratorially to one another, obviously not believing a word. "Where does Erning live?" He says he doesn't know; all he remembers is being scared, Jessilyn not waking up, knowing for certain he would be blamed for it, deciding it's better to just give himself up.

"What does he look like?"

Tall, he says, a big man, fair skinned, with straight hair. I stop and think a moment before the next question. "Did you like Jessilyn—you know, like a girlfriend? Like some people are saying? Enough to get jealous if you saw her going out with someone else?" *No, never,* he says, and his eyes mist over. *I've known her since she was a little kid, her mother would sometimes ask me to keep an eye on her, playing in front of my shed while the mother ran errands. They trusted me, the whole family. I would never have hurt her.*

In the back of my mind something is itching. The caretaker at the Methodist compound heard her cry out once. If Elmer's first confession were true, the girl might have been too far away from the compound to be heard at all.

The monkey has fallen quiet, having finally found a comfortable perch on the windowsill. As we prepare to leave, I look at his face in repose: he stares blankly into the room, and I realize he and Elmer have exactly the same color of eyes.

THE COMMUNITY HOSPITAL is not far from the police station. We drive there in Tony's car. Dr. Cabigting is on leave, all right, for "personal reasons." We ask for her address, wait half an hour in a lobby that smells faintly of soured milk, in the middle of wailing babies and stoic mothers, their breasts drooping from past childbirths. A nurse hands me a piece of paper with the address; I fold it up and put it in my pocket.

Tony begins walking toward his car. "What the hell is going on here?" I say to him, and it probably sounds like I'm holding him responsible for the shitshow I've walked into.

He spins around slowly. "A murder in a small town. Everybody related to everybody else. Lots of little secrets." He resumes walking to the car, and I follow.

"Come on, Tony, you're not Jesus. Don't speak in parables. Am I in over my head here?"

"Never stopped you before." He unlocks the car door.

The heat from the metal raising the hairs on my arm. "Well, fuck you."

He throws his camera bag in the back, slams the door. "Listen, Joanna, you're not stupid. Just don't impose any logic on this thing because there won't be any."

"He couldn't have done it, right? Am I right here? Does he look like a murderer to you? Could he put her down fast enough so she could cry out only once?"

"What do you want me to say?" He goes over to the passenger side, holds the door open. "Get in the car. Come on," impatiently now, "I'm not asking for a blow job."

"In the next Ice Age, I would blow you." I slide into the seat, grumpy; the seat is like one big hot-water bottle.

"That could be sooner than you think." He gets in, slams the door, turns up the air conditioning, drives off. "Give me the address." I take the slip of paper from my pocket and give it to him, close my eyes, let myself drift off for a while.

"There's a few ways you can look at it," he is saying now, his voice floating toward me through the haze of drowsiness. "Either it's just a bunch of provinciano idiots who don't know which end is up. Or it's one big, orchestrated cover-up. Or it's both, and the first one makes the second one easier for whoever is pulling the strings."

I don't look at him but I am thinking: Tony's mind is light. Not butterfly-light or empty—light like an electrical impulse shooting down a circuit board, endlessly free-associating, seeing connections, permutations, variations the way other people see little green men sitting atop lumps of earth in their backyards. He has looked at Jessilyn Samson's death and drawn an infinite number of possible conclusions, *Elmer guilty, Elmer not guilty, Erning guilty, not Erning, somebody else, one assailant, two assailants, three, she knew him, she knew them, she didn't know him, she didn't know them, the cops involved, the mayor involved, the health officer involved, not involved.* The facts we know are itching in his mind like trained fleas, some lining up obediently under one conclusion, not in the next, here in another.

I wish I had a mind like his. Instead, my mind is slow and heavy, sitting in the dark like a massive albino toad with red eyes, waiting for some cold and awful truth to pass, edible, before it.

Tony reaches over, takes something from the glove box, tosses it in my lap. "Seen the examination report?" I nod. "You know more about forensics than any layman I know. That fancy French school you went to. Tell me what you see." He is trying to shake me out of drowsiness or confusion or both.

"Forensic anthropology. An elective. And I've forgotten most of it." I unfold the papers. "Okay. She took a hit in the head. Bruises on the arms and wrists, right shoulder dislocated. Cause of death, asphyxiation." I shuffle the onionskin pages. "No indication of whether the assailant was left- or right-handed."

"But *you* have some idea." He maneuvers the car deftly

over the rough dirt road, avoiding goats and rocks and tiny, dirty, half-naked children.

"My guess, left-handed. Says here the bump was on the right temple. Would have been simple enough to tell assailant's approximate height and weight if they had done X-rays—fracture lines from the point of impact can give you that." I look down at the autopsy report. "Two vaginal swabs."

"Two?"

"And two separate findings, one negative for sperm, the other positive, that's one for the books." My eyes go round, and I flip through the pages, turning them over and over again in search of an explanation that I already know won't be there. "Right. Don't impose any logic. I hear you. Okay. No samples from under her fingernails. No samples of the dirt on her skin."

He takes his eyes off the road a moment to look at me. "I'm guessing you want to get this Dr. Cabigting bad."

THE DOCTOR IS not home. She is not at her daughter's home; not at her cousin's home; not at her elder sister's home. The doctor is nowhere near Posadas. We finally trace her to Baticuling, at her *other* elder sister's home, at around six in the evening, the sun beginning to go down. It takes her a while to come out to the sala to face us. When she does, she's a small, round woman in her midforties, short hair, wearing a white T-shirt (*San Ildefonso Bowling Tournament '95*) and one of those mock-suede stirrup leggings from Hong Kong that do nobody any good to be seen in. She seems nervous, although from duress or from mere fear of being found incompetent I can't tell.

"You performed the examination on Jessilyn Samson?" Yes. "Could you describe the state of the body?" She describes the body the way it is in the photographs, the arrangement of the clothes, the stains down the front of the jeans, the bloodied mouth. "Can you explain the dislocated right shoulder? The hematomas on both shoulders?" No to both questions. "Did you take any samples of dirt from beneath her nails?"

"No, I did not her fingernails." She drops a verb somewhere on the floor of her mind; I have a feeling there are a lot of things lying in little piles on the floor of her mind.

"But if she scratched her assailant, you could match the samples from beneath her nails with samples from a suspect. Right?" Tony shaking his head, *useless to ask these questions*. I ignore him. "Okay. The swab results you sent to the NBI. Two swabs, two results, can you explain this for me, please? No? Right, the lump on her temple. Did you examine it further? No?"

"Joanna, stop."

But I don't stop because I'm angry and I'm on a roll. "How about the dirt on her skin, did you scrape off any samples? No samples? Her clothes, what happened to her clothes? You put them in a bag? What kind of bag, a plastic bag? Okay, the clothes, what did you do with them? You sent them with the body to the funeral parlor? You didn't keep them? You don't keep the clothes *ever? Even in wrongful death?*"

I take a deep breath, so deep it makes me dizzy for a moment. "Dr. Cabigting, how many times have you performed this function before?"

"Many." *Many times.* I look at Tony, and some of the helplessness I feel must be written on my face because he speaks to the woman for the first time.

"Why did you go on leave?" She looks blankly at him. "Why did you go on leave?" He asks the question louder this time, and he's stern.

"Oh." She pauses a while. "I am visiting my relatives." It's the only question she seems to have a ready answer for.

"Did anybody ask you to go on leave, Dr. Cabigting? Because we had a difficult time trying to find you. Why didn't you leave word with your own family, the members of your household?"

"No. I am visiting my relatives." It comes out smoothly, like she's practiced it a hundred times before inside her head, ready for just this moment and just this question.

The sky completely dark now as we get in the car to head back to Posadas. My head hurts; I didn't get much sleep last night. "Logic, Joanna." Tony's voice, quiet, but with that edge I know so well. "Chuck logic. Chuck procedure, chuck the things you know or you think ought to have been done. You won't find them here." They're the last words I hear before I fall asleep.

HE SHAKES ME awake. "Get your stuff."

"What?"

"Your stuff. You're checking out of this dump. You can

take my bedroom instead." The door on the driver's side slams shut and he moves over to my side. I mumble in protest but do not move. "Wake up, Joanna, you don't want to be here when the D'Licious crowd starts to get down and boogie-oogie-oogie."

My limbs are stiff from the air conditioning and the cramped space. Already he's disappeared into the motel. I step onto the sidewalk and stretch my legs for a bit, wriggle my arms, listen in satisfaction as my joints crack.

From down the street, the sound of a car engine, very loud, the vehicle going very fast, and seconds later I see a patrol vehicle, or what looks like it, an owner jeep with very big wheels, an antenna, an array of big round flashing lights just above the windshield. The wheels churn up dust into the air, and I see the thing coming toward me in a red haze, coming close so close *Jesus Christ watch it* then swerving in a tight curve to avoid me, stopping heartbeat inches away from the nose of Tony's car, tires squealing like pigs to the slaughter.

"Wow, Miss Beautiful!" someone shouts. I can't make out the face in the darkness, but I can tell he is smiling, that malicious half smile worn by people who think they know things about you. Before I can answer the vehicle is off again, roaring down the street in a swirl of dust, and Tony is rushing out of the motel.

"What the hell was that?"

"I don't know." I cannot feel my knees.

"Did you see their faces? Could you recognize them if you saw them again?"

"No. And no."

His jaw is set, lips in a thin, grim line; he doesn't take his eyes off the street. "Stay in the right hotel, you get popular really quick."

TONY'S BED IS very comfortable, clean, soft, firm. He's developed a taste for the good life from years of living in five-star hotels, and his mattress is proof of this. He has brought me home and fed me and then trotted off to the living room with spare pillows like a good little gentleman. His bedroom walls show a side to his work I've never seen before: black-and-whites of women's bodies—just bits of them, hands, mouths, feet, breasts, ears, buttocks. It is difficult to make out what's what at first; he has photographed them so that skin looks like sand, undulating in the heat of a desert.

"This is all very sick in here," I holler, and he comes back into the room, padding softly on bare feet.

"What, don't you have any of those?"

"Women are more than the sum of their parts."

"The parts are more than just bits of the whole." Any pride he might have taken in these photographs has vanished, leaving only a kind of defeat; I can read it in his sagging shoulders, the resignation on his face. "It's the architecture, Bonifacio. You have to look at their fundamental architecture." I know my face looks like I just sucked on a lemon, and he's too tired to explain further. "Ah, what's the use, you're a goddamned Philistine. Go to sleep."

• • •

THIS MORNING WE are going to see Jessilyn's folks in Cacdang, a small farming community not far from Baticuling. The drive is dusty, dirty, and hot; we stop every half hour or so to ask for directions. After what seems like an endless succession of fields and carabaos and coconut trees, we find the Samsons' neighborhood. The car has to inch its way along a narrow dirt road with deep ruts and large rocks; split-bamboo fences hug the road on both sides, and at one point Tony wonders aloud if the paper will reimburse him for the paint job he thinks the car is going to need afterward.

The Samsons live in a cluster of homes behind one such bamboo fence. In the cluster are three or four nipa and wood huts built close together. Chickens and children roam the yard freely; Jessilyn's relatives in Manila told me that five families live here, all related to one another. These same relatives wrote ahead to her parents to expect us today. A small group of adults greets us at the entrance to the compound.

"Where is Emma?" I ask for Jessilyn's cousin, who is our contact person here. She steps forward, and I blink once or twice; her resemblance to Jessilyn is astonishing. When I look around and actually pay attention, I see Jessilyn's fine features and clear skin on more than half a dozen faces. I feel as though she is here, watching me.

Emma brings us to the hut of Jessilyn's parents. Tony is snapping away; the children gather around him as though he were a movie star, smiling for the camera, eager to get in the shot. The door is low and I have to bend to get through it. The parents stand deferentially as I enter; their faces are worn and lined, and so are their hands, stiff and dry and scarred by a lifetime of hard, unrewarding work. I see traces of Jessilyn in the shape of the mother's face, in the set of the father's eyes.

In the sala, a stack of tacky photo albums is waiting for me, bits and pieces from Jessilyn's nineteen years. The three of them wait without speaking as I wander with eyes and fingers through the photographs; *there*, they seem to be saying, *you can see for yourself what we all know, that she was a good girl, a happy girl.*

When I am done with the albums, Emma hands me Jessilyn's diary.

"Do the police have a copy?" Yes, but they did not do anything about it. The cousin with Jessilyn's face shakes her head in silent reproach.

The diary is written on loose, unlined sheets of paper, folded in half. Jessilyn's writing is tiny, typical of young girls documenting their small, ordinary lives in script so minuscule as to discourage prying eyes.

I take my time reading; this, in gloriously broken English, is Jessilyn, even more so than the photographs. This is how she lived; this could tell me how she died. The time I spend poring over it is punctuated only by the occasional cackling of a hen in the backyard and the shuffling noises of her relatives at the door, some leaving to attend to chores as others take their place, watching us.

Elmer is mentioned several times in the diary. Elmer selling three chairs at one go and buying pancit from the nearby carinderia for the family supper, to celebrate an unusually good sale. Elmer asking Jessilyn to buy him some glue and string in town one day; asking her to write and mail a letter for him on another. Elmer cannot read or write; I am not surprised.

Under the date February 24 comes this entry: *Sir Ning has given us restaurant staffs an extra three hundred bonus from his winning.* Jessilyn used the money to buy a new watch, the watch she was wearing when she died. And later, under the date March 19: *Sir Ning have ask us to sing in his b-day party. There will be a combo.*

On the twenty-fourth of March: *I have go home with Helen by tricycle; the jeep of Sir Ning is repaired.* The spelling was bad, but that wasn't why reading on hurt: it was that almost everything that happened in her life was there, so open and guileless. All her extra income, down to the last centavo, which mostly went to her family. All the little get-togethers where she wore her best dress (*white with blue polka dots*) and ate spaghetti and drank pineapple juice. All the petty quarrels with girlfriends that were quickly patched up within the next few pages.

Under the date June 2: *I am so happy. I have a brand-new maong pants for Mayor Adi's b-day. I will ride Sir Ning's jeep with Helen, Tet and Margie.* The mayor's birthday was June 3rd—the whole plaza had been appropriated for the celebration, long tables groaning with food, a makeshift stage and a sound system, gift wrapped prizes for a raffle. Jessilyn would not live past the wee hours of June 4th.

The Posadas police have their own copy of the diary. If

I had been the investigating officer, I would have checked on everybody mentioned in it, on his or her whereabouts on the night of the murder. But I wasn't, and they didn't.

"Who is Sir Ning?" Emma says it is the owner of the restaurant at the cockpit. Jessilyn took the orders of customers and totted up their bills, as did the three other girls she worked with. The name sounds awfully close to Erning; I wonder if the police have made the connection, if they have even followed it up. Tony thinks this is the same man the police picked up and released almost immediately.

We take our leave of Jessilyn's parents, of Emma, who has been to Manila and will not sit as meekly as her aunt and uncle grieving over the loss of her cousin and accepting it as God's will. No; Emma's eyes mist over with tears as we go, but they remain wide and defiant: *somebody must pay.*

Out of Cacdang and back toward Posadas, Tony and I are both quiet, Jessilyn real in our minds. When Tony finally speaks, I am far away. "We can have lunch there."

"Huh?" I ask stupidly.

"Lunch." He lifts his right hand from the steering wheel and wiggles his wrist, to draw my attention to the time on his wristwatch. "It's three o'clock. We haven't had anything to eat since this morning."

I nod, even though lunch is the last thing on my mind. "Where?"

"The cockpit restaurant," he says.

About an hour later, we drive into a large compound bounded by a well-made concrete and wire fence. A few other cars are parked near the fence on the inside, and Tony follows suit, pulling into a parking spot just underneath a coconut tree. We get out and look around. The compound encloses several structures, the largest of which is an octagonal cockpit with a green dome and sturdy wooden benches along all eight sides. The place is cool, and all around me is a strange but soothing sound, a whooshing that seems to underscore every other sound I hear, from the singing of birds to the padding of our feet on the grass, and it occurs to me it is not just the wind. It dawns on me that the place is not just a cockpit; it's an entire resort, and the green grass under my feet eventually yields to pebbly soil, which in turn grows smoother until it becomes pale gray sand.

"That's the sea," I say, and Tony points helpfully to a line of coconut trees just ahead: a few more meters and I find myself looking at the ocean, fiercely blue and shimmering under a blazing afternoon sun. I catch my breath and stand still for a moment. Tony touches my arm briefly, indicating the small, nipa-roofed restaurant to our right. I turn and follow him.

A plump, pleasant-faced young girl shows us to a table with a good view of the beach. Tony orders grilled fish and seafood and two Cokes. When she goes off to relay the order to the kitchen, he turns to me. "I'll translate." I nod; the girl comes back with our drinks.

"What's her name?"

Tony asks her; she says, "Helen."

"Ask her about Jessilyn."

She smiles sadly. *Yes, she was my friend, she worked here. Did she have a boyfriend? No, she was a quiet girl, she only* went out in groups; if she had had a boyfriend, we would have known. How about suitors, somebody who was interested in her? *There were a few men; Jessilyn was pretty. She mostly kept to herself, though; she wanted a chance to get back into school. She had quit two years before graduating and she wanted to save money to start her studies again, to tide her folks over while she paid for tuition.*

"How about your boss?"

At the mention of her boss, something changes in her face: the sad smile is still there, but something in the eyes, a flicker of something darker, fear or alertness. *Sir Ning? He is very nice to us.* Did he like Jessilyn? *He is married. He is very nice to us.* Did the police talk to him? *Yes, but he went home at once. He is very nice to us. I'll see if your fish is ready.*

Tony and I exchange glances. He pours a measure of Coke into his glass of ice and drinks it down. A few minutes pass, and then someone comes from the kitchen with two platters, steamed rice on one and a large grilled fish on the other. We look up at him; he is smiling at us.

"Hello." He sets the platters down and holds out his right hand to Tony. "I'm Ernie Sta. Maria. I own the restaurant." He shakes Tony's hand and then mine. His hands are large, and so is he, tall, on the heavy side, a little over two hundred pounds, I estimate; fair-skinned with Chinoy features, in his mid to late twenties. There is something familiar about his face; I cannot put my finger on it. He is wearing a white T-shirt with short sleeves, blue jeans with their cuffs rolled up at the ankles. I have never seen biceps as big as his.

"You were asking about Jessilyn."

"Yes," I say, "we're covering the story for the *Observer*. Perhaps we could ask you a few questions."

He pulls up a chair and sits at the table companionably. "Jessilyn was a nice girl. We never had any trouble with her. She worked well and never complained about the long hours. You know, sometimes the special derbies end at one, two A.M." It occurs to me that he smiles too much for someone who is talking about a dead person. I glance at Tony; the look in his eyes, cool and measuring, tells me he has noticed it as well.

"We understand the police questioned you about the murder."

"Oh, yes. They thought I was the person her cousin was accusing."

"Did you and Elmer ever come face to face at the police station?"

The smile stays on his face but goes dead in his eyes. "The police released me because there was no evidence."

"But did you see each other?" I'm not going to let him get away with not answering the question.

"Well, even if we had seen each other, there was no reason for the police to hold me. It was his word against mine, and he is not mentally sound." He taps his temple with the forefinger of his left hand, then twists around and signals to Helen with the same finger for the rest of our food before turning back to us. "I think Elmer was in love with her. Did you read his first confession?" We nod. "Poor Jessilyn. She was a good girl."

"Did you bring her home that night?"

"Yes, as usual. I drive the girls home whenever I can, it just makes sense. Elmer picked her up from the entrance near the Methodist church, like he always does."

"Around what time was this?"

"Well, you know, I've already told the police all this, but, let me see, it must have been around eleven, eleven thirty. These girls are like daughters to me. Take care of your workers and they'll take care of your business, right?" If he's looking for some sign of affirmation, he doesn't get it from either of us.

"Yes, Jessilyn talked about you in her diary." It's the first time Tony has spoken, but the effect on the other man is astonishing: the smile has left his face and he seems to have gone gray underneath his pale skin. "Didn't the police mention her diary? It's very detailed."

Sta. Maria clears his throat and begins drumming the fingers of his left hand on the wooden tabletop. "I think Elmer's confession was sufficient." It is the answer to another question, one that is obviously on his mind as well as ours. Tony pretends not to notice, and I follow his lead.

"Did you like Jessilyn?"

He turns to look at me. All pretense of friendliness is gone and, in its place, a coldness and hardness in his eyes. "I'm a married man. I take care of these girls. I pay them well."

I meet his gaze and hold it, hoping that my face betrays neither hostility nor fear. "If new evidence turns up, there could be a reinvestigation."

Helen arrives with a plate of shrimp and mussels; Sta.

Maria reaches for the plate, lays it on the table, and stands up. "Well, I have to go. Enjoy your meal." He disappears into the kitchen without another word. In a few moments, we hear from somewhere behind the kitchen the sounds of a car being driven away at great speed.

We stay quiet until the sound of the engine dies down, and then I ask Tony: "Should we worry?"

"We should eat."

After our meal, he suggests we walk along the beach. The sun is a bright orange disk in the sky. I take off my sneakers and wade into the water, Tony walking ahead of me and skipping stones expertly on the surface of the waves. It is the one half hour of peace I have had since I arrived in Posadas, although Jessilyn continues to hover in the back of my mind.

Coming up from the beach at the end of our walk, I look down at my bare feet; the sand is hot.

The sand. The gray sand, with its pieces of broken shell.

"Tony." It comes out as a question.

He looks at me, at my feet, at the sand, and says nothing. He knows no answer is necessary.

IT IS NEARLY seven when Tony and I pull into his garage. The car is covered with a thick film of dust; on the windshield are two fan shapes where the wipers have cleared the film away. We trudge into his home, Tony kicking off his shoes as he goes along, and I collapse on the couch. He heads for the answering machine and plays back his messages.

"Hello!" The voice is female, friendly, familiar. "I'm leaving a message for Joanna Bonifacio. Hi! I'm Melinda Ochoa! I was informed that you were in town covering the Samson case!" Every sentence ends on a high note, as though she were greeting friends at a cocktail party. "My husband and I would *love* to have you over for dinner tonight. Can we send somebody to pick you up? Okay, I'll see you later! Bye!"

Tony's face is grim. "You have a knack for making new friends."

"Adi Ochoa's wife," I say.

"Thank you, I live in this province, I know who she is." I open my mouth to reply but he suddenly motions for me to keep quiet. We both hear a car pull up outside the gate, two, no, three. One of them starts honking its horn, and then I hear car doors slamming shut, and footsteps on the pavement, then the doorbell. "Stay here."

"No," I say.

He presses his lips together tightly, then walks out the door; he knows better than to insist. I follow him.

A sleek silver BMW is parked alongside the curb; behind it and in front, two Toyota HiAces, both black. A man is leaning on the side of each van, and I can make out the shapes of other men in the vans' windows. Two men stand just outside the gate; they smile as Tony approaches, but I know they are all armed. Tony asks them a question in the dialect; the mayor has sent them to pick us up for dinner.

Tony turns to look at me. *You could refuse*, his eyes tell me. I stare back at him: *next time they ask, they won't be so nice.*

• • •

ADI OCHOA'S WIFE, the former Melinda Barredo, was a beauty queen who drifted into the movies and show business in the late eighties, as most beauty queens do. She met Ochoa during a campaign sortie in the provinces, where she'd been invited to sing and dance and get the crowd hyped up for candidates from the political dynasty to which she'd soon hitch her wagon. The Ochoas are rich and powerful, the perfumed and polished lot of them, and unspeakably corrupt. But to Melinda, that was just an inconvenient fact, like Adi's two prior marriages, his very public flings with very beautiful women, his dozen or so children, legitimate and otherwise. She herself has given him two young sons, both of whom will eventually take their place in the dynasty's pecking order.

Melinda Ochoa is small, with delicate features on flawless morena skin. Her hair cascades over her shoulders in soft waves, managed no doubt by a small army of expensive hairdressers. When she meets us at the door, she hugs me as though we were old friends, and Tony snorts quietly; he knows I can't stand people invading my space—especially people I've never met before in my whole life.

Adi, former congressman and now the mayor of Posadas, expert horseman, business tycoon, is nowhere to be seen. Melinda's quick sharp eyes see me looking for him. "He's been called away at the last minute. You know naman, even in a small town like this, there are so many problems."

She leads us through the living room, waves us through

sliding glass doors to a patio that has been set up for a small dinner party. Maids in blue-and-white-striped seersucker uniforms bustle about. The service table, on the right side of the patio, is heavy with food, too much food for just three people: egg-drop soup with fresh pepper leaves in a deep wooden bowl; mounds of grilled pork belly; huge steamed prawns and mussels; large mud crabs split in half and sautéed in garlic and butter; a salad of tomatoes, fiddlehead ferns, and crumbled kesong puti; deep oval platters heaped high with garlic fried rice. For a moment I wonder if there are any other guests, but it soon becomes apparent that all this obscene bounty has been organized solely for our benefit.

"I always thought Joe Bonifacio was a man, I thought you would be this big macho guy," she gushes in her colegiala English. "And then I saw you last year on TV asking the president a question and I said to Adi, 'Oh my God, he's a girl!'"

I nod, trying my best not to roll my eyes. Ah, my glamorous career as a political reporter, all five months of it. I pick at my salad and bite my tongue.

"And now I finally meet you! You should really drop the "e" from Joe! And I didn't expect you would be so tall," she continues, her pretty face lit up with a sincerity so false that she has tricked herself into actually meaning it. "You know, I've always been fascinated by women journalists. You have Amanpour, you have Walters. Such an exciting life!" Women journalists, wow. I hate that. I hate being called a woman anything. How come nobody ever says, *Oh, I'd like you to meet Mr. So and So, acclaimed man journalist?*

I give her a small smile, and thus encouraged, she prattles on. "You know, I used to read your work in *View*. Sayang the magazine, what happened to it?"

"Basically nobody read it, is what happened to it."

I notice she doesn't address Tony, *he's just a photographer*, but Tony doesn't mind. I can almost see the gears turning in his head. Poor Melinda Ochoa, she might shrivel up in embarrassment if she knew how well Tony reads people, how he can see past her colegiala affectations and her effervescent chumminess, the studied casualness of her blue jeans and short-sleeved shirt, trophy mistress of a filthy rich man living the oh-so-simple life in this rural backwater, in a home designed by a Japanese architect, the occasional flash of one or two well-chosen diamonds on the fingers of her constantly mobile hands. She would be mortified if she knew that Tony saw, so clearly, how she was merely tolerated in her husband's family, how hard she tried to fit in and be nice to her domineering snob of a mother-in-law, mastering the skill of relentless flattery, trying and never quite succeeding. How well she took the occasional beating from her hard-drinking husband. How she looked at all of it philosophically, how pragmatic she was about it, how artfully she applied concealer to the bruises, small prices to pay for living well.

"But *I* read it," she whines now in her girlish voice, as though *View* should have stayed in print just for her. "So sayang, and then you used to have these ganda pictures of the tribes in the mountains, the cave dwellers, how dramatic pa with the fog and the mist and everything."

"I guess we tried to be *National Geographic*, but *National Geographic* got there first." Tony nearly chokes on his soup. See, that's why I don't think of myself as a journalist, because my pretensions are far loftier: I was an ethnographer for *View*. And no, she isn't the kind of person who would have read *View* willingly, unless it happened to have been among the courtesy reading material on a plane trip she took or lying around in her dentist's waiting room.

"Pero you know," and now she leans toward me, reaching out to touch my arm as though sharing a confidence, "I hope you will be objective about this murder thing, ha." So here it is at last, the stick after the carrot, the real reason why we've been invited here. The words lie on the invisible table of conversation like a live mudfish, wriggling, black, slippery. "My husband has many political enemies who would not hesitate to use this against him."

It's awfully difficult not to jerk my arm away like I've come in contact with a boiling kettle, but I manage to hold it steady on the table. "Oh, but I don't think we're here to crucify anybody. The thing we're concerned about," and this is me trying to be calmly rational, professional and reassuring, yet not yielding too much, "is that all of these people—the police, the hospital—none of them seemed to know what they were doing, and that reflects quite badly on the mayor."

"Ay, you know, that's *so* true," she sighs, shaking her head. "Sometimes he's blamed for things he knows nothing about! But many people really do not like him, because he's tried *so hard* to get rid of the corruption and the vice here. I think even the police, I think there was some conflict with the police when he first assumed office. So, you know, it's really hard to get their cooperation on *anything*."

I take a long sip of water before I go on. Think policy-related issues, think good governance and best practice, all the jargon and catchphrases that paper over the slime and the sewage and the blood this town and this family are built on. Think anything but that this whole thing reeks of a cover-up and I think your husband is behind it or else we wouldn't be here, eating your egg-drop soup and your fern salad and your garlic butter crabs. "I'm hoping the article will highlight any areas that need to be improved in the administration of the town, because really there's too much going on for one man to handle. The case is important only because it illustrates some of the shortcomings of the local government. Which are not entirely in his control, of course."

It's all bullshit, but I'll say anything she wants to hear, if it means Tony and I make it out of this place alive.

She leans back in her seat, relief spreading over her face. "Ay, I'm so glad," she says, as if I've settled something that's been bothering her. "You know, that will be *so* helpful to him, getting an outside opinion." She's been afraid, I can see it: afraid for her husband, afraid of the possibility of a scandal touching, poisoning her precious, perfect little world. But she's not dumb; she might deny it, but she knows only too well that everything around her is already poisoned, her diamonds poisoned, her cars and clothes and designer bags poisoned, her life and her children's lives poisoned. But the poison is so delicious, so addictive, it's impossible to even imagine going back to living without it.

A door opens and we all turn to look at the man who has just stepped into the patio. He is in his late forties, broad shouldered, just shy of six feet. He doesn't swagger, but he wears the unmistakable air of someone accustomed to being obeyed. Adi Ochoa is a formidable presence, and when he enters a room, conversations tend to cease. I should have remembered this; God knows how often I had seen him while I was still on the *Observer*'s political beat.

"Hi, honey," Melinda calls out cheerily. He turns, gives us the barest nod of acknowledgment then crosses the length of the patio and disappears down a flight of stairs into the garden. Only when he is gone do I realize something else: his face is a face I have seen before, a face I have seen just this very day. Save for the sag under the eyes and the slack at the jaws, it is Ernie Sta. Maria's face.

Sta. Maria. *Adi Ochoa's mother is a Sta. Maria.*

It is all suddenly so clear: Ernie's infatuation with the pretty Jessilyn, the alcohol that flowed freely at the cockpit during the mayor's birthday celebrations, the perfect opportunity to make his feelings known to this girl, this chaste girl, this unresponsive girl, this terrified girl who had to be kept quiet. The need, throbbing, searing, not to be denied, only to be satisfied one way or another, down at the beach where her cries would be drowned in the thunder of the waves.

Thinking quickly now, putting her in the jeep. Driving her, unconscious but alive, to her temporary home just like every other night. But she wakes up, she cries out. Quiet, keep her very, very quiet. The ensuing panic, the fatal miscalculation in that cramped space.

Now her half-wit cousin, stumbling through the foliage: the perfect fall guy.

The powerful uncle who would make everything all right.

Everything but Jessilyn, dead in her new jeans.

I look at Tony. He is already there. He has been there all along, and so has this entire town. Our eyes lock in terrible, dangerous knowledge.

Melinda Ochoa turns, smiles, and for the first time in the evening addresses Tony directly. "Sweet the prawns, *no?*"

THE FUNERAL PARLOR is a series of small, ramshackle wooden structures, one leading to another, leading to another. They are roofed with rusty galvanized iron and stand on a lot devoted to the cultivation of weeds. A few people are standing outside the lot, whispering among themselves by the side of the road. We walk past them.

The man who comes out to greet us when we knock and call out is dressed in tattered brown shorts—actually, old pants that have been cut at the knees and left unhemmed—and a sleeveless undershirt that is startlingly white considering what he does for a living. Either the shirt is new, or his wife loves him very much.

Tony lapses into the dialect, introductions all around, then on to business. "Did you prepare the Samson girl for burial?" The man nods, polite but watchful. "Who brought her here?" The police and the family, straight from the hospital after Dr. Cabigting was done with her. He waits while Tony translates for my benefit.

"Did they bring her clothes?" Yes. "Where are they?" He asked the police to return the clothes to the family after dressing the dead. "And did they do that?" He said he was told to just throw them away.

The man asks us to follow him, first into a section of the structure obviously used by his family as their living quarters, then farther into the innermost section, where he embalms the dead.

The wooden door creaks on its hinges. In the center of the room stands a very large slab; on closer inspection we find that it is not one whole piece of rock but hollow blocks and mortar slapped together. On top of it is a flat, rectangular piece of metal about two by six feet, depressed in the middle from the weight of the bodies it has held, its four edges turned up an inch or so, a large hole at one end. It reminds me of something, and then the hairs on the back of my neck stand as my mind makes the connection: it looks like a giant cookie sheet.

As Tony begins to click away, I look around the room. It is almost empty; strangely, I can see nothing else in it to suggest the sort of procedures that are routinely performed here. There is another door in the back of the room; from beyond it I can hear children's voices, splashing water. It is odd, hearing their laughter from in here.

"Ask him what they do with—you know..."

"The bodies," Tony finishes when I hesitate. He asks; the

man says they are washed in the back before being brought in here. Tony turns to me again; *want to look?* I nod.

But this time the man refuses, even before either of us has said a word; he says that someone is waiting outside for his turn at the table. This explains the people waiting by the roadside.

Another realization: the children are playing and bathing in the same area. The man reads this thought in the dismay on my face. He explains unapologetically and with some amusement *there's only one faucet.* Tony takes me firmly by the elbow and leads me out of the room, through out to the side of the road.

"I'm okay. Why, do I look sick?"

"No, but this is the reality of life out here. One home, one tap, and that's if you're lucky. You're judging the place and he can see it."

"I'm doing no such thing."

"Well, whatever it is you're doing, stop it or we won't get anything out of him." Tony turns to the man, who has followed us outdoors. "What do you think she died of?"

"She was strangled. But he didn't use a rope."

Tony's eyes light up; he translates for me, and then asks: "What, then?"

The man balls his hands into fists and brings them close together with the thumbs sticking out. Then, he spreads his legs and bends slightly at the knees, clenches his fists, and bears down heavily on some imaginary throat with his thumbs. The dislocation of her shoulder, the hematomas, the bruises on her neck inconsistent with ligature marks made using a rope, all of these become clear in an instant: the man had knelt on her shoulders, pinning her down, while his powerful hands crushed her windpipe.

A tall man, a heavy man, a little over two hundred pounds, who could put down a tall, healthy nineteen-year-old girl fast enough so she could cry out only once.

When we get back to the car, I take the wheel while Tony sketches with a pencil on a sheet of ruled pad. This is the way we now see the murder in our eyes: Jessilyn on the ground, a man kneeling astride her torso, pinning her down. I've seen Tony's drawings before; usually his hand sketches in light, feathery strokes. This drawing is different; the strokes are dark and heavy, the composition jagged, frenetic. He encloses the figure of the man in a series of circles, then draws a big question mark above them.

"So," I begin. "Her injuries were inflicted by someone bigger, heavier than she was. Can we get Elmer released on what we know about how she died?"

"We could try to have her exhumed. But a court wouldn't recognize you, and a court wouldn't recognize the undertaker."

"An expert, then." I take my eyes off the road for a moment to look at him. "We could find an expert."

Tony falls quiet. He lays the yellow pad on his lap; the pencil rolls off it as he looks out the window on his side. A couple of kilometers of monotonous scenery pass by before he talks again. "Joanna, how long are you here for?"

"I've got till tomorrow, I guess. Why? I can get my flight moved to the next day if I have to."

"And then what? Will the paper send you back here to do a follow-up?"

"I don't know, it depends—"

"Joanna, do you know what you're doing here?"

"Excuse me?"

"I said, do you know what you're doing here? Are you writing a story or *solving a case*?" The vehemence with which he asks the question almost makes me jump out of my seat. He's so exasperated with me, I'm afraid he might rupture an artery. "What did I tell you yesterday? Chuck logic. You want to dig her out? Dig her out yourself. You want an expert opinion? Find a box big enough, bring her to Manila. Or you can bring your expert here, underwrite his expenses. You want to get Elmer released? YOU do it. You work the phones, you grab the shovels, you do the legwork, you find the money."

"Why are you jumping all over me?" It comes out as an accusing whine.

He takes a deep breath, summoning patience. "What I'm saying is, you're not some hotshot detective, Joanna. So just do your job. You're too late to save Jessilyn and you can't save Elmer. You can't hunt down the faceless bad guys and throw them in jail. You can't straighten all the crookedness out of this fucking town. You have enough to worry about just doing your job."

I steer the car onto the road shoulder, stop, turn to him. "I'm not an idiot, Tony. I'll admit it took me a while to figure out what you already knew, but I figured it out anyway. What was that you said? A murder in a small town.

Everybody related to everybody else. Was that your way of telling me? I was a bit slow on the uptake, but thank you, I'm all caught up now. I know they've handled things so that he will never go to jail for it." Out of frustration, I slam the palm of my hand down on the horn. The blast of sound makes birds fly out of the scraggly trees nearby, beating their tiny wings as though in startled anger.

It is nearly a minute before I take my hand off.

We sit in silence, in the heat radiating off the vinyl dashboard and the PU leather seats, in the muggy air that wraps around us, clinging to our damp skin.

"I know all I can do is write it."

"And I'm saying . . ." He takes a deep breath, then leans forward and rests his head in his hands, as though he has a monumental migraine. "I'm saying that will have to be enough."

MY FLIGHT IS at 10 A.M. Tony drives me to the airport; it is tense and awkward in the car, as though we are suddenly strangers again. Every once in a while, one of us will say something, about the weather, about airport schedules, about the photos which he will have to send in the mail, and the other will nod, grunt, say yes or no. He pulls into the parking lot of the airport, and we sit in the car without talking for a few minutes, staring straight ahead through the windshield.

"Damn it, Joanna." How do I respond to that? I don't know, so I keep my mouth shut. "We were just too late."

"Yep." We both get out of the car. He helps me with my

bags, and we proceed to the departure area. I check the bags in and make sure I have my ticket.

"Well, I'll see the story when it comes out, I guess." We both linger. He looks smaller than ever now, and I realize I am seeing him in a moment when he feels so very small, so completely powerless. I feel the same way, hobbled, hands tied: knowing what we know, knowing that nothing we can do about it will ever matter.

Without another word, I turn around and make my way to security. I know he's still waiting, but I don't look back.

BACK IN MANILA, I write a story about a girl who is raped and murdered, about the one cry that precedes the silence of her death, about the town that keeps justice from her. It's long enough to hack into three parts for three consecutive issues; my editor runs it with Jimmy Soria's series on the inefficiency of police in rural areas, some eye-watering stats, a few sample cases of world-class bungling. Jimmy is the paper's most senior crime reporter; he says the Samson case, unfortunately, could be the rule rather than the exception. I think about that for a long while until I can't think about it anymore, because it will eat me alive.

By the time the series wins an award for investigative reporting, I've left the journalism game, comfortably ensconced in an air-conditioned office in a Makati high-rise, handling corporate communications for a company that produces financial software.

This is how it ends.

In many dreams, the girl walks toward me, coming

through the black in her T-shirt and jeans, the stains down the front, the dirt on her skin. In these dreams, she holds out her hands, empty but for grains of sand and grit and tiny fragments of broken shell. She asks no questions with her bloody mouth and makes no accusations with her dead eyes. The open hands say all, all: *What now?*

The phone call comes months later, just as I'm starting to forget, just as I've deluded myself that I'm starting to forget. It comes in the middle of the night, with me lying in bed, restless but exhausted from my comfortable new job and my comfortable new paycheck and my comfortable new life.

After I put down the phone, I sit up in bed, in the cold stillness of my room. *Nothing we can do about it will ever matter.* The albino toad opens its red eyes and looks into the darkness, knowing.

I GET TO the PNP morgue just after the body is brought in. The bag is made out of heavy black rubber, and zips down the middle; even with it closed, the odor is unmistakable. How long has it been, six months? Eight? I hesitate at the doorway. What am I doing here? Over and over since Jessilyn Samson died into my life, I have asked myself that question. Today she is going to give me my answer.

Somebody taps me on the shoulder; I turn and see Tony. He looks the same as usual, but odd somehow for being here, in a city he hates.

"Just starting?" he asks. I nod, step aside a bit to allow him to pass. We stand side by side in silence for a moment, and then he turns to me. "You don't have to stay, you know."

"I know." From another door at the end of the room, Fr. Augusto Saenz enters; he is a Jesuit priest who is regularly consulted by local law enforcement agencies for his expertise as a forensic anthropologist. Years ago, he was my anthropology teacher at a Paris university; he sees me, nods in recognition but does not smile. There is nothing to smile about in this room, in all the rooms like this, with work like this to be done.

The priest is dressed in a white smock, to protect his clothes. He fishes a pipe from his pocket, checks the bowl, lights up; the sweetish scent of tobacco smoke masks the odor of decay, but not entirely: the treacherous smell asserts itself again and again.

Tony and I feel awkward in each other's presence. I clear my throat, then say: "You managed to swing it, somehow. The exhumation. Elmer's transfer to another facility, away from Posadas."

"You kidding? I've dropped your name so many times, I should use it to get a bank loan." I feel something ease between us, like I used to feel as a child, toothache gone after a trip to the dentist. I know that's about as much information as I'm going to get out of him now, and probably ever, though I have a nagging suspicion he's somehow tracked down the investigating officer who was so conveniently reassigned before I arrived in Posadas a lifetime ago. Maybe some people are still capable of telling the truth in this fucked-up country.

It's only a little past seven in the morning but I am looking forward to the end of this day, the long day of Jessilyn's death. She probably won't be able to tell us much more than what we already know. Certainly not enough to keep the man who killed her from getting away with it. But maybe just enough to keep the man who didn't kill her from paying for it for the rest of his life. It's a small justice—a half justice—but a necessary justice all the same. Sometimes that's all we can hope for; most times that's all we can get.

I wrote a story. That's all I could do. But here she is. And here we are.

KEEPING TIME

The door of his hotel room is open; the porter has stowed his bags and is now hanging up the contents of his suit bag in the closet. Mike enters the room sideways, sucking in his gut. It is an old habit; even though he has shed more than a hundred and forty pounds, he still feels like a fat man. Sometimes he catches himself doing it; when he does, he backs out of the door and comes in again like a normal person.

The porter closes the closet door, stands aside with a deferential smile. Just like him, falling into old habits. Mike takes a large bill from his wallet. The porter is briefly stunned, then flashes him a broad smile. "Thank you, sir."

Mike nods, says nothing. The door closes behind him and he is alone.

He is bone-tired—six countries in seventeen days—but there's still work to be done. He unlaces his shoes, sets them aside in one corner of the closet and pads around the carpeted room in his socks. He finds his laptop bag, plugs the machine into an outlet, begins undressing as it boots up.

Having lost all that weight, Mike tends to take better care of his clothes—mainly because he now has better clothes to take care of. Although his job has always paid well, he never bothered much about his clothing or appearance until the weight started coming off a little over three years ago. These days he always dresses well; even after long-haul flights, he arrives at meetings immaculately turned out, as though making up for decades of self-loathing and neglect. On site—where weather, ground, and even social conditions can be unpleasant at best and downright treacherous at worst—he takes great pains to dress appropriately, to remain as clean as humanly possible.

He hangs up his jacket, shirt, and trousers carefully; he'll have them dry-cleaned tomorrow morning. He strips off his socks, roots around in the closet for a laundry bag and puts the socks inside. He'll take a shower and brush his teeth before buckling down to business.

In his bare feet, the transition from carpet to the chilly marble tile of the bathroom is a bit jarring. He doesn't particularly care for the paper slippers that hotels provide—there is something silly and ineffectual about them. So he takes the cold floor like a man, without complaint or fuss.

In the mirror above the capacious sink, he sees a stranger.

For the better part of nearly five decades, the man in the mirror was always overweight, ballooning to some three hundred and forty pounds around seven or eight years ago. He was tall—well over six feet—and he had a nice enough face. But the face grew jowly and shiny from sweat, and he couldn't bend far enough to cut his own toenails. At some point, he tipped from pre- to full-blown Type 2 diabetes. He learned to exit conversations quickly when the discussion turned to his weight or change the subject when even the most well-meaning of relatives told him "You'd be so handsome if only . . ."

He used to be married, but she left him when he broke the three hundred pound mark, when he couldn't maintain an erection and his sperm count dwindled. This, too, he took like a man, shrugging off the sympathy of family, friends, colleagues, going about his work with the same implacable precision, the same clinical detachment. In private, he ate his way into numbness, a lumbering giant laced with deep and invisible scars.

Now, at forty-seven, he is the man he has always wanted to be: muscled and trim, save for a little residual fat around the belly and love handles, and under the arms. With his looming physical presence, intelligent eyes, and silver hair, he looks distinguished, attractive, if a bit icy. If his wife were here, if they had just met, she would be all over him; he is now the exact type she would have found irresistible. She has been dead several years now, though, one of the first to go.

He studies his image.

He might as well remember himself like this. It will not last long.

BACK IN THE room he checks his office email. There are fewer and fewer people left at work now, and his workload seems to have grown exponentially over the past four or five years. It's evident from the number of emails he has received in just the past seven hours—the time it took to fly from one country to another, retrieve his baggage, clear immigration and customs, get to the hotel from the airport, check in, freshen up.

Inbox: seventy-two unread.

Most of the emails have to do with the same thing: the water problem. It's always the water problem now. Everywhere he goes, he always finds the same damn thing. It's in the water, in the rain, in the rivers and lakes; it cannot be dammed up, it cannot be stopped. The inhibitor only slows it down, but its spread and its effects are largely irreversible.

Always a different country, always the same story. Mike feels like the angel of death, arriving on the scene only to tell people what they already know, confirm what they already suspect.

He reads the emails but decides the replies can wait. A glance at the bedside clock tells him it's nearly 2 A.M.

He turns the lights off in the bedroom. Clad only in his pajama bottoms, he steps out onto the balcony to smoke. He has only recently taken up this vice; there's poison enough in his system not to have to worry about adding a little bit more.

He leans against a wall, lights up, takes a long, slow drag, blows out the smoke in a series of tiny white puffs. He hasn't yet learned the right configurations of lip, tongue, and mouth needed to blow smoke rings, and these little puffs are as close as he's ever come.

Beneath an inky sky, the city is quiet, its stillness punctuated only by the occasional bleat of a car horn or rumble of a train. The cities of his youth—Manila, where he was born, New York, Tokyo—were bustling, noisy, claustrophobic with their great masses of people. That's all just a memory now. The world's biggest cities, and its smallest, its poorest and wealthiest—all are in the same boat: half their populations wiped out, the other half just waiting for the inevitable. If not for the computers running farms, manufacturing, logistics, transport and communications, power grids, the planet would have ground to a halt years ago. That'll happen soon enough.

The sliding door to the adjacent balcony opens, and a woman steps out. She has left a light on in her bedroom, unlike Mike, whose balcony is shrouded in darkness. He is happy to observe her, unobserved. With the hotel virtually empty, she has not bothered to put much on before venturing outside: she is wearing only a pair of black satin panties. Her back is turned to him as she talks softly into a mobile phone.

Mike catches fragments of her end of the conversation—something about a funeral, about not being able to go, how sorry she is. Her voice is low and raspy, as though she hasn't spoken to anyone in days. Even from behind, Mike notes that her body, bathed in the dim amber light from the bedroom, is in very good shape. It does not have the usual sag and droop that usually afflict fat people who lose vast amounts of weight in a relatively short time. He decides she must be relatively young, her skin still elastic. He focuses too long on her backside and does not realize that her telephone call has ended.

When she turns around, the first thing she sees is the tiny pinpoint of fire at the end of his cigarette.

Mike starts, his breath rattling out of him. He is unprepared for the way she looks: darkly beautiful, with a haunted face, her long hair only partly covering her breasts.

A natural courtliness finally kicks in and he steps out from the shadows; it would be better, he thinks, not to be perceived as a Peeping Tom. He prepares to introduce himself, to be polite, to shake hands, but his throat locks just as he is about to say hello.

She steps back, crossing her arms over her chest, her mobile phone resting on her right breast. In an instant she turns and disappears into her bedroom, the sliding door clicking shut, the light going off.

Mike feels an odd sense of disappointment and something else—a sensation of disequilibrium, like stepping off after a harrowing roller coaster ride. He retreats into his unlit room, closing the door to the balcony. He is not breathing right, and his head feels suddenly too large, too heavy for his body.

He finds the bed in the dark, lies down, breathes slowly and deeply; but the feeling will not go away.

He has to touch himself before he can get any sleep.

HE'S SUITED UP for the morning's ministerial conference at the WHO. He has all the briefing material ready: photographs and footage, statistics, firsthand accounts, lab results. Some of it is extremely technical; all of it is horrifying.

As he is about to step into a waiting hotel taxi, he catches sight of the woman from the room next to his. In the daylight, she looks to be in her midthirties, although there is something about her manner—gravity, watchfulness—that suggests to Mike that she could be older. She is wearing dark slacks, a matching jacket, waiting for a car just like his. When it pulls up in front of her, she sees Mike, recognizes him from the night before. A blush suffuses her face, but she holds his gaze steadily for a moment before she disappears into the vehicle.

At the conference, all the faces Mike sees are grim. About a third of the people in the room are in the final stages of wasting: emaciated, eyes bulging out of sunken sockets, bellies distended, clothes hanging off their bodies. They move slowly and with great difficulty, some hooked up to parenteral nutrition drips. When this conference reconvenes in three months as scheduled, many of them will not be in attendance. The world's best minds in public health, their ranks thinning inexorably.

When it's his turn at the podium, Mike spends a few moments booting up his laptop, flipping through his documents. The eyes that look upon him take in how normal—how good—he looks. There is envy, and there is also a certain mild derision: *you must have been so fat*. He has learned not to let this get to him.

Always a slight flutter of nervousness before he speaks at these events. Once he begins, it will go away. He clears his throat, adjusts the microphone to suit his height, introduces himself.

"Good morning. Good to see you all today. I'm Michael Tejada and I'm a field investigator for the World Health

Organization." He switches on the projector, skims the audience with his eyes before proceeding. "I'll be taking you through the major findings of our surveys in the Asia Pacific region for the last three months."

His words are thoughtful, measured; unnecessary, really, to dramatize the awfulness of things. He paints a sobering picture of the places he's been to, what he's seen, tests he's run. The photographs, charts, and tables on the screen behind him cause the audience to lapse into a stunned and dismayed silence.

It had all started in North America, and it should have stayed there. But there was money to be made, and Europe soon followed suit. It was a simple process, the drug companies said, just like fluoridation.

Conventional wisdom held that Asia should only have started feeling the effects of the problem much later. But Mike's research shows otherwise. Many in the region had clamored to have their water treated, citing rising rates of obesity, heart disease, hypertension, diabetes. But vanity was just as great a motivator. Given the massive demand, some governments had secretly tested the enzyme on domestic water supplies, only to find they could not contain it. The contamination spread, tainting supplies like a ferocious algal bloom.

Children and the elderly are always the first to go. Pregnant women pass the enzyme on to their unborn babies, and they begin starving in the womb. If by some miracle a child is born alive, its DNA is already hardwired for starvation.

By the time the first wave of deaths hit the Western Hemisphere, much of Asia's water was already irrevocably fouled. Soon, Mike tells the group, the entire region will be grappling with the problem—even countries whose backward water systems had somehow insulated them from the contamination so far.

After Mike speaks, other experts step up. One talks about the legal ramifications of the crisis. Class action suits continue to pop up all over the world, but the company that synthesized the enzyme and licensed the technology to the pharmaceutical giants has long gone bankrupt. And the governments that agreed to the treatment have resorted to legislation to protect themselves from claims, on the premise that financial resources should be allocated to seeking a solution.

Mike is supposed to be part of the solution. But as one of the lead investigators, and the one with the most comprehensive knowledge of the situation on the ground—four continents, sixty-three countries and counting—he knows there is none. All that can be done is for the drug companies to manufacture as much of the inhibitor as possible, dump it into water supplies and hope it can delay the inevitable. The scientists can find ways to boost its efficacy, but not by much. At most, the planet has seven years before all its water supplies are wholly contaminated, either by the enzyme itself or by the inhibitor.

Even in this, Big Pharma continues to make Big Money, most of which will never be spent.

The ultimate joke, perhaps. But no one is laughing.

• • •

MIKE EATS A solitary dinner at the hotel's Italian restaurant. Loading up on carbs and protein helps to slow down the decline, and he finds himself in the ridiculous position of having to eat to keep his weight up. The restaurant is nearly empty except for him and a couple at the other end of the room, their plates also piled high. He had hoped that his boss Peter could join him; but he, too, is in the final stages and can hardly get out of bed. Coming to the conference today was pure agony for him. Mike had told him to go home.

The woman walks into the room: navy blue skirt, white blouse, arms bare, hair loose. When she sees him, she stops in her tracks. Mike senses she is trying to decide whether to stay or leave. When she turns and goes back the way she came, Mike wipes his mouth, throws his napkin on the table, and follows her. In several long, quick strides he is close at her heels.

"Wait," he says.

She walks faster, turns a corner to get to the elevators.

"Wait," he repeats, louder this time.

She's almost running now, and he's brought up short by a trolley half-laden with baggage, pushed along by the porter from the previous day. The woman darts into one of the elevators. She looks at Mike; considering that she has just fled from him, she appears surprisingly unruffled. The elevator doors close before Mike can get to them.

"What's the point of running," he snarls. "I know where to find you."

HE DOES NOT see her anywhere in the hotel the next morning, before he heads to Peter's home. He had considered knocking on her door last night but decided against it.

On the drive to the gated community where Peter lives, Mike sees all the signs of contamination: the abandoned buildings, the half-empty streets, the shuffling skeletons on the sidewalks that look like they were displaced from Biafra in the late sixties.

Peter Darrow has never been fat, but he has always been tenacious. Even now he clings to life the way he has always clung to his convictions; he has a job to do, and he'll die doing it. With little energy to climb the stairs, he has taken to sleeping in a room on the ground floor of his two-story house. Only a nurse and a cook attend to his needs now— his wife and two grown children are dead. He is sitting on the edge of his bed and just about to have breakfast when Mike arrives.

"I'm sorry, would you like me to wait outside?" Mike asks.

"Sit, sit," Peter insists, waving him toward a nearby chair. There is a plate stacked with pancakes on a folding table in front of him, another plate of sausages on the side. "The dietitian keeps telling me to pack it all away. You want some?"

Mike shakes his head, drags the chair over the floor, and sits across from Peter. "No, thank you. I did my own packing away this morning." Even from this relative distance, Mike can smell his boss's breath, rank from catabolysis. A plastic tube snakes out from under his T-shirt, attached to a bag filled with intravenous fat emulsion. He's not yet at the point where the body begins to reject any amount and type of nutrition, but he'll get there within weeks.

The older man begins to eat: stabbing at the pancakes, chewing with neither hunger nor pleasure. "Always thought eating was a waste of time. Sleeping, too. Now I hardly do anything but."

"You're joking, right? You still email me a dozen times a day, riding my ass."

Peter flashes a puckish smile, and for a moment he looks as he did seventeen years ago, when Mike first came to work for him. "You're a good kid, Mikey. I had a great team, and you were the best one in it. You were smarter, worked harder than anyone else. And everybody on that team worked *damned* hard."

He's already thinking in the past tense. A sound escapes Mike's throat, unintelligible but unmistakable: a welter of emotion trapped there. Peter recognizes what it is, wisely decides to ignore it. Between the two of them, words aren't necessary.

"So where are you off to next? Polynesia?"

Mike regains his composure. "Kiribati, Samoa, Tuvalu. The reports aren't good."

"There haven't been any good reports since this whole business started." Peter sighs. "The Age of the Enzyme. Bigger than AIDS. Badder than bird flu. You can't vaccinate it away like COVID or stop it at the source like climate change."

Mike sits quietly for a moment. "Peter, I have to ask. Who takes over when you—I mean . . ." It's not easy to find the right words, or the right words are just impossible to say. The crusty old Brit is more than just his boss; he is mentor, friend, surrogate father. He is also one of the last surviving of the world's leading epidemiologists.

"When I croak?" Peter pushes the sausages around on the plate; their oily sheen only sickens him. "Arief Hasnawi from the Eastern Mediterranean. Theophile Allegre—he has little enough to do in Europe, it's too late for them. Terry Chen from the Western Pacific—he still has a good two, maybe three years left in him. You, I have to keep on the ground. You're not an administrator. I need your sharp instincts out in the field. While you're alive and able to function, my friend, you're the timekeeper of the world."

Mike mulls this over for a while. The three men are nowhere near as experienced or single-minded as Peter, but they will have to do.

"The turnover's likely to happen before the next conference. I'm sorry I won't be around to help you, old boy. You'll do well, I know it."

Mike does not know what to say, so he says nothing.

Peter pushes the plate of pancakes away; he's barely made it through a fifth of them. "Listen, Mikey. Can I give you some advice?"

"Always."

"Don't be alone when the end comes. That's key. Everything else is just noise."

RESTLESS IN BED, Mike stares into the dark.

In the Bible, the Angel of Death is a messenger; the Talmud says he appears when there is no further remedy to be found, no other appeal to be made.

Timekeeper of the world.

Mike closes his eyes, tries to will himself to drift away. *Let this cup pass from me.*

For years now, he has denied his loneliness, has refused to even think about it. When his wife left him, it was easy to blame the weight and move on. The last few years, struggling with the demands of work and an escalating global crisis, have made it very easy to forget.

Tonight is different. Something, maybe despair, maybe hope—they can seem so alike—stirred inside him on the balcony the other night. It has gnawed at him these last two days, and it refuses to be stilled.

He hauls himself out of bed and ponders his situation for a moment. It is possible she might call security; it would be embarrassing, but he is unlikely to be thrown into jail for simply knocking on a door. She could answer and then merely close it again. That's all right, he decides; he's used to doors closing on him. Would she open it, let him in? Strangely enough, this seems the most disquieting prospect.

He glances up and down the hall to see if there is anyone coming or going. He feels a bit foolish for doing so; he is a grown man, after all, and the hotel is quiet at this hour. He pauses to collect himself, and then rings the bell. It's well past midnight, and she is likely to be asleep. He fights the urge to scuttle back to his room and rings the bell again.

He hears shuffling on the other side.

She does not seem surprised to see him.

"Hello," he says. She says nothing, waits. "I'm in the room next to yours. My name's Mike."

The question, when it comes, is polite but somber. "What can I do for you?"

He hears a sound that might be the hum of the hotel's air conditioning or the rush of blood to his head. "I'd like to talk."

"Because?"

"Because." He pauses. "Because I can't sleep. And obviously, neither can you."

The door closes; for a moment Mike thinks it has closed for good, but he hears the clink of the chain being undone. When she opens it again, she is alert but not wary; she steps aside to let him pass. There's only one lamp lit in the room, framing her in its warm orange glow. She is wearing a white tank top and jeans, her feet bare on the carpet. When he brushes past her, he catches a whiff of citrus, her perfume or shampoo. Her laptop, blinking on the dressing table, plays music.

"I don't know what to call you."

"Marisol."

"Hello, Marisol." Now that he's finally in the same space with her, he feels as unsure of himself as a schoolboy. Her gaze is fixed on him, following his every movement. He gets the sense, for the first time in a very long time, that someone can really see him. It is simultaneously unnerving and exciting. *Say something, anything.*

"Why did you run away from me last night?"

"You want the truth?"

"Truth's always nice."

"Not always." He can sense embarrassment in the way she breaks eye contact. "I suppose the same reason you were running after me."

"Ah." Mike feels a rare stab of pleasure. He knows what it's like to run from the very thing you want.

"I saw you yesterday," she volunteers after an awkward silence.

"Outside the lobby, yes. I saw you, too."

"No, at the conference."

"The WHO conference?" He is taken aback. "What were you doing there?"

"I'm covering it for my agency. I caught your report. I've been following all your reports the last few years, actually. You've been very busy."

"Ah." Mike tilts his head slightly. "I didn't see you there."

"I tried to stay out of your way."

"Because of the other night?" She says nothing. Mike looks down at his feet. "I scared you *that* much?"

"You scare me now."

He clears his throat, suddenly dry. "That wasn't my intention. Isn't."

"What *is* your intention, then?"

The laptop is now playing a familiar song. When he

recognizes it, he can't help but smile; it seems ridiculously appropriate for the occasion. "*Par la contradiction de ma tête et mon cœur*," he echoes softly. "*J'en deduis que je t'aime.*" The look that flickers across her face tells him she's pleased.

He walks toward the balcony, pausing a short distance away from the glass doors. They're open a few inches, and a mild breeze is stirring the curtains. He is aware that she is still watching him closely; he hopes she is not repelled by what she sees.

"My wife is dead," he says quietly. "Well, she left me first. Then she died."

Without seeing her, he can tell she's moved a bit closer to him. "In the first wave?"

"Yes." He laughs a bitter little laugh. "The one that killed all the supermodels."

A moment's silence. "Did she see you before she died?"

"No. I'd wanted her to. So she could see what she gave up." He shrugs. "In the end, there didn't seem to be any point." He is surprised to hear her laughing softly. He turns to look at her. "Share?"

"There was a man once. I suppose you could call it a mercy fuck. He whipped out a calculator after sex, tried to figure out my BMI. Said I would be so pretty if . . ."

"*If only you lost weight,*" he joins her in finishing the sentence. She blushes, somewhat embarrassed but not displeased. Strange, how such a little thing can seem so intimate.

"Well. I was doing a story on the water problem last year—about hospitals here not being able to cope. He was a patient at one hospital. He was in the last stages. He saw me."

Mike can't help staring at her. If she had looked anything like this last year, Calculator Man would have been beside himself.

"What did he say?"

She has a habit of glancing away before saying something uncomfortable. "He said: 'And the fat shall inherit the earth.'" Her tone is dispassionate, her voice steady. Something tears inside him.

"He was an idiot."

She touches him first, unsure, her fingers lightly brushing the hair on his arm. She does not meet his gaze, focusing instead on the point where her fingers meet his skin. When she withdraws, he quickly moves in: locking his powerful arms around her, pressing his body hard against hers. He feels resistance ripple through her, but he refuses to let go, brushing his lips against her hair, breathing her in, and that resistance soon ebbs away. He spreads one large hand over the small of her back, lets the other drift to her waist, under her top. His heartbeat quickening now; her skin is smooth, so very smooth. He lays her on the bed, holds her firmly in place beneath him.

"Listen to me," he demands, forcing her to look at him. "There are no calculators here. Listen. He was an idiot, okay?"

When she finally looks at him, she does not break eye contact. "A dead idiot now," she says, and then neither of them says anything for a while.

• • •

LATER, SHE SITS away from him on the edge of the bed: a little island, close but not too close, her back to him. She does not seem interested in the customary post-coital cuddle. Perhaps that will change someday; he would like very much to find out. Right now, he feels the need for a cigarette. He has a few sticks and a matchbook in the pockets of his sweats. "Do you mind if I smoke?" he says, reaching for them where they lie on the floor. She shakes her head.

He lights up, takes a drag, does the choo-choo train thing with tiny puffs of smoke. She watches his reflection in the mirror on the dressing table, in that same soft, unblinking, mildly unsettling way, and he feels compelled to explain himself. "I'm trying to learn how to blow smoke rings. Right now, they just come out like this."

"You don't like it when people look too closely at you." It's a statement of fact, not a question.

"It's a fat person thing. You would know."

She laughs gently and he's relieved she's not offended. "Yes, I suppose I would." She shifts position on the bed. "At the conference you said the clock is winding down."

Mike walks over to the sliding doors, opens them wider to let the cigarette smoke out. "Six years. Maybe seven."

"So we're all screwed."

"Are you going to quote me?"

"*Speaking to this reporter after a round of bone-rattling sex,*" she intones solemnly, "WHO *public health expert Michael Tejada said the entire human race is basically fucked.*"

"Bone-rattling. I like that." A pause. "You wouldn't be misquoting me. Total contamination of water supplies will take about seven years, but most of us will have starved to death by then."

Even as the words come out of his mouth, he wishes he could take them back. But she chews on it for a while, then shrugs. She beckons him back with the merest tilt of the head. He grinds the cigarette into an ashtray on a nearby table and climbs into bed beside her. She touches his face with both hands, as if learning every line and feature by heart.

"You're beautiful, for a dying man."

HE IS ROUSED from sleep by the sound of her moving around in the room. She is dressed and done packing. He speaks slowly, not fully awake. "What time is it?"

"Seven A.M." She is tying her hair back into a ponytail.

"You're going somewhere."

"Water riots in Istanbul. Flight leaves at around nine. I'm running late."

He lets this sink in a moment, watching as she wheels her luggage to the door. When she opens it, she lingers in the doorway, half in, half out.

"I'm flying to Kiribati tomorrow." He extracts himself, half-naked, from a tangle of bedsheet and blanket, and moves toward her. "And after that—well, I'll be moving around a lot." He hopes he doesn't sound desperate. Not too desperate, anyway.

"Same here." She strokes his cheek with the back of her hand. "What are you trying to tell me?"

He takes a deep breath, bows his head, and closes his eyes. In his mind he runs through a number of responses, some sweet, some smartass, all lame. He thinks about Peter's advice, about what's key, about how everything else is just noise.

In the end, he settles on the simplest, the most truthful answer. "That there's so little time left."

She bends, pressing her cheek to his, her fingers brushing his silver hair. They hold each other a long moment.

"There'll be time enough to teach you how to blow smoke rings," she whispers.

THE GYUTOU

It was only a kitchen knife, but as far as knives go, it was museum quality, collector worthy. It was a Gyutou made of the finest carbon steel: layered, lightweight, and with an impossibly sharp edge. It was born in the forge of a Japanese artisan whose family had been making knives and *katanas* in Seki for centuries. Like a child born into royalty, it knew it was not like any other knife. It was not even like any of its brothers and sisters born in the same forge, and it knew it was meant for great things.

Above all, it knew that a knife with its heritage deserved only the greatest pain and the tenderest of ministrations.

A knife of the Nozaki workshop is born the same way as all its predecessors have been for the past four centuries. The Maker takes more than sixty pieces of hard and soft steel, puts them through flame and ice, pulls and stretches and hammers them until each layer melds into the others. Each piece imparts its own anguish to the finished blade, and by the alchemy of fire and water, this chorus of agony becomes a single coherent voice: the soul of the knife. The blade is then ground down, sharpened on waterstones of ever finer grit and polished until it acquires a mirror-like finish: smooth on one side, patterned with irregular grooves on the other. Its tang is set in a handle of dark ebony wood, fixed in place with rivets of polished brass. The finished knife is a thing of fearsome power and beauty.

The Gyutou had known only two other pairs of hands in its life; first, the cruel but noble hands of his Maker; next, the gentle, knowing hands of the Woman. It was she whose hands had spoken to its knife's soul, whose name it bore in gold kanji lettering on its blade.

The Gyutou first heard the Woman's voice in its Maker's store. Its heart of steel had quickened at the sound, and with its blade—which was its eye, its ear, and its skin all in one—it had tried to gain a sense of her. She was not Japanese, she was not white; she was something it was not familiar with. And though she spoke the language it knew as English very well, there was something else in her speech—a lilt, an accent—that the knife had never heard before.

The Maker had sent a young assistant to translate for him, and she began to tell him what she was looking for: something very sharp, with a blade patterned like damascened steel, a full tang running throughout the length of the handle for balance and strength: something light, but substantial in the hand.

What will you use it for? the Maker had asked respectfully; for a woman who knew to come to Seki to look for a knife knew exactly what she wanted in that knife, and knew which knife maker to look for, deserved that knife maker's respect.

Ordinary things, she had said. *A loin of tuna, or of pork. A crisp cucumber or a ripe pear.*

She said it with a note in her voice that stirred the

Gyutou's heart of steel. Unlike the ordinary stamped blades made in factories or at the forges of inferior craftsmen, knives like it longed for the day when they would learn their true Purpose. This Purpose gave meaning to their early suffering: why they had to endure the scorching flames of the forge, the jarring cold of ice water, the angry blows of metal that came after or in between, and at the end, the searing acid that stamped the Maker's name on their blades.

For many such knives, their Purpose was to be collected and admired, for they were truly works of art. Others were employed in the preparation of food for paying customers or the residents of palaces. The most fortunate ones were used in the homes of families, where they became an essential part of everyday life. And then, inevitably, there were knives destined for violence and bloodshed. A knife would deem itself most unfortunate if it counted itself among the Desolate, as such knives were known.

The Maker took a tray and thoughtfully laid on it a selection of his best knives, their blades ranging from 6.7 to 10.6 inches in length. Each kind bore a different name. The *sujihiki*, a long, narrow blade used mainly for slicing. The *santoku* or "three virtues," which could be used to cut meat, fish, and vegetables. The *usuba*, best for fruits and vegetables, and its double-sided sibling, the *nakiri*. The *honesuki*, a boning knife with a heavier blade. And the *yo-deba*, heavy and used mainly for butchery and harder vegetables.

At last, the Maker took the knife from its display case and laid it on the tray along with the others.

This, he said, *is a Gyutou. It can be used for many things: vegetables and fish, fruit and meat, even bread. It is best for the home and despite its size, it is suitable for a woman's hands.*

And this was how the knife got its first glimpse of the Woman. She was tall, with black hair and smooth brown skin, large dark eyes, neither too thin nor too fat. She was not beautiful, not even merely pretty.

But something in her face held the Gyutou's steel eye. For many people came to the Maker's store, and many looked preoccupied, or haunted. Others were in a hurry, or greedy to buy one of his treasures. The Woman's face was unlike all these. In it, the Gyutou read the purest joy: for she had come a long way to find the perfect knife.

Is love to be my Purpose? the Gyutou asked itself.

The knife soon became aware that one of its brothers—the largest of the three Santoku on the tray—was eagerly trying to catch the Woman's eye. It preened, it gleamed, it flashed its brilliance so that it would be chosen. But the Gyutou sensed that the Woman was not one to be dazzled. Instead, it mustered all its inner fire, but tempered it with the memory of its pain, and its fond hope of serving her, so that she saw only its noble character and luminous warmth.

Her fingers alighted on the Gyutou's ebony handle, and it felt electricity ripple through each layer of its blade. Her touch was gentle but sure, cool and warm all at once. The joy in her face turned to quiet contemplation; she tested the knife's weight, passed it from one hand to the other, ran a forefinger across the grooves of its blade.

After a few moments of reverent silence, she turned to the Maker and the assistant and said: *this one*.

The Gyutou was taken away to feel the burning acid for the last time, as it traced her name on the reverse of its blade.

THE GYUTOU TRAVELED with the Woman to a new place, far from Seki. This place was her home—a densely packed city of skyscrapers and squalor, of wide highways and slow traffic—yet they were both outsiders here.

For the next five years, the knife's home was a drawer in a sunlit kitchen, in an apartment the Woman shared with a man whose food she prepared each day with the finest knife she could find. Although she worked outside the home, she always found time to make his meals. In time the Gyutou learned to recognize the names of the dishes it helped her to make. If the man asked, *what are we having for dinner*, she would answer, adobo or nilaga, haemul pajeon or rendang.

The Gyutou quickly learned which dishes would require the chopping of many vegetables, the slicing of meats, the filleting of fish. It knew that preparing a sandwich meant cutting square slices of bread into triangles for easier eating. It learned that there was ordinary bread and there was good bread, the kind that was crisp on the outside but held sweet, chewy softness within.

In mere weeks, it learned flavors and colors, textures and smells: the tang of lime, the tough shell of pumpkin, the yielding orange translucence of salmon. It even knew when there was company coming; there was always so much more work to do. But the Gyutou never felt weary, because it could feel excitement and anticipation and a genuine desire to please coursing through the Woman's fingers and pulsing through each of its many layers of steel.

In this city, where so many lived hand to mouth and everyone always seemed to be in a hurry, the Woman resisted by living her life slowly. She read books under what trees she could find, walked to the supermarket, took her time in the produce section. She did not crowd her hours with ladies' lunches or high teas or cocktails, where people put on nice clothes and even nicer airs, networking and building contacts. Her address book was not crammed with business cards and phone numbers. The few people she allowed into her life were there, not because they were useful or could advance her career, but because they mattered to her. This, after all, was a woman who would travel to another country to buy a kitchen knife.

This same deliberate slowness and care marked the Woman's relationship with the Gyutou. Every time she used it, she would clean it immediately and slip it back into its sheath and box. Its ebony handle was dried thoroughly if it had been exposed to moisture; every month, the Woman would treat the wood with mineral oil to keep it from cracking or warping. If the knife was used to cut acidic fruit, it was immediately rinsed and wiped so that its blade would not dull. Occasionally, it would be sharpened on a special waterstone the Woman had also purchased from the Nozaki workshop.

These rituals would be performed even on days when

she was tired, or ill, or in a rush. The knife was never carelessly handled or tossed into a sink or drawer with other hard objects. It was never left exposed to the elements. Had the Gyutou a voice, it would have told her that the Maker's art was such that one, two, or even a dozen lapses would not be sufficient to dull or nick its blade. But it was deeply moved by her concern and respect, and vowed to honor them with its loyalty and service.

But it felt differently about the man. Although he too was careful with the Gyutou, it was a care born out of the knowledge of its price, and not its worth. More importantly, the Gyutou felt very early on that the man was not worthy of the Woman's devotion.

An insurance salesman who never seemed able to close a deal, he stayed home and watched television all day. He rarely helped around the house; he left dirty dishes in the sink for her to wash even though she put in a full day's work and would come home tired. When she asked him to do something, it would take him weeks to get around to it. Often, she would either forget that she had asked or get tired of asking and end up doing it herself. When she tried to plan for their future together, he would become evasive and irritated. *Things are fine just as they are*, he would say. *I'm happy with what we have.*

And only the Gyutou heard the Woman as she whispered: *But I am not.*

BEFORE SHE MET the man, Samantha's life was an endless whirl of parties and clubbing. She was a young woman of means, but detached from her family. She shopped, she drank, she hooked up, perpetually searching for something that neither retail nor alcohol nor sex could provide. She joined a church band, where she met the man. She latched on to him even though he was about two decades older, because she liked the thrill of landing an older man and even better, she liked the idea that she was attractive enough to break up a long-standing relationship. With the rest of her life spinning out of control, she liked the feeling of power that she got from destroying something.

She hooked him in, first by introducing him to the trivial amusements of young people like herself: instant messaging, social networking—all the tools and interests that would give them common ground and bring them closer together. She called him at odd hours of the night, asking him to pick her up from clubs where she had once more drunk herself into a near-stupor. She dug her claws in deeper by telling him that she had once been hit by an ex-boyfriend. And she made sure to tell him that he was the only person in the world that she had entrusted with this secret. *I have no one else*, she whimpered to him over the phone in her little-girl voice, *you're all I have.*

The man was selfish, and weak, and so unhappy with himself that he needed to rescue someone just as troubled and unhappy as he was, to feel alive. He was consumed with a desire to protect her, so powerful that he forgot everything, including the Woman's loyalty and devotion.

But he did not realize how easy it was to read a faithless

man. The Woman had seen all the signs: the strange new software installed on his computer, the endless hours he spent chatting on the internet, the vagueness with which he now referred to unnamed "friends" when he said he was going out. His sudden interest in new places, new music, new websites recommended by these new friends. His lack of enthusiasm for interesting places the Woman had discovered during her wanderings and hoped to share with him.

The Gyutou felt the heaviness in the Woman's heart: in the uncharacteristic slowness of her knife strokes; in the simmering anger with which she sliced at a piece of meat or hacked at a head of cabbage. But more importantly, it felt this in the progressively longer periods it would sit in its sheath, in its black box, unused.

Through its many protective layers, in the darkness of a kitchen drawer, the Gyutou soon heard the muffled sounds of change and upheaval and sorrow. It heard her usually soft footfall quick on the tiles now, rushing from one room to the next. It heard the slamming of closet doors, the sound of newspaper being ripped and crumpled, the crack of duct tape ripped from a roll. It was that time of year called Christmas, and for the first time in five years, there was no cooking, no music, no laughter.

The day the Gyutou last felt the Woman's touch, it knew it would never see her again. She was dressed in her going-out clothes, and she was eerily calm. She opened all the kitchen drawers, surveyed her beautiful plates and fine stemware, the pots and pans she had each selected for different uses, the cutlery which she had chosen with such great care, and let her fingers linger gently over them for the last time. *I'm sorry,* she whispered, *I can't take you with me.*

At last she came to the Gyutou, which she reverently removed from its box and unsheathed. She said nothing but grasped it as though seized by some mad, awful impulse. The Gyutou was alarmed, for this was one of the ways that a noble knife became one of the Desolate: when humans turned their blades against others or against themselves.

But the moment passed, and only the Woman's tears fell on the blade. They burned into each groove of the layered steel, and the Gyutou felt a new Purpose stir in its soul.

The Woman put the knife back in its sheath, in its box, and closed the drawer. And then she was gone forever.

LESS THAN A week later, the knife was rudely shaken out of its sheath by Samantha's rough hands. It fell with a deep clang into the metal sink and was doused with running water before being used to hack away at a frozen pizza.

This was the beginning of the Gyutou's misery. Soon, it would be subjected to all manner of abuse. This new woman was young, impatient, did not know how to cook a meal or keep a clean house. And so the knife was pressed into service not just for frozen pizza but also for scraping mold off the bathroom tiles and soap scum off the kitchen sink. It was never returned to its black leather sheath and its textured black presentation box but was left instead to air-dry in treacherous humidity. Once, it was left on the kitchen counter overnight, unwashed and exposed after the young woman had used it to cut a lemon.

Since it was no longer sheathed and boxed at night, the Gyutou soon became aware that other things in the apartment were conscious like it. It came to understand that these things too were imbued with the memory of her. Objects of cast iron, copper, and stainless steel, though made of metals not as noble as its own, had retained her imprint as the Gyutou had. So, the knife was amazed to learn, did objects of ceramic, plastic, cloth, and glass. And while they did not question their Purpose like the knife did, they too struggled to comprehend how their fates could have changed so quickly and so terribly.

In time, Samantha became increasingly suspicious that things were not right in the apartment. It started with little things: a glass slipping out of her hands, a mild shock when she plugged the microwave into an electrical socket. Then a mirror on the living room wall crashed to the floor for no apparent reason, breaking into a thousand fragments.

Within a span of three months, three glasses out of a set of six had leapt to their deaths from the young woman's blighted hands. A glass pane from one of the kitchen windows nearly impaled a cat several floors below. When Samantha tried to use the gas stove, flames suddenly leapt three feet into the air, singeing some of her hair. She never used the stove again.

She had complained to the man that the Woman had accumulated too much junk. All that stuff in the kitchen—*we can always eat out!*—all the beautiful bed linens, the little treasures in the living room, all so unnecessary. *Can't we have a modern, minimalist little place, so chic and luuuurvely?*

But privately, she sensed that something did not want her here, knew she had stolen the space she now occupied.

She did not know that the man, too, had begun noticing things: how the light bulb in the refrigerator exploded, how the heater in the shower yielded only icy cold or scalding hot water. How plates that were stamped "microwave safe" cracked or melted in the microwave; how the supposedly long-lasting bulbs on the living room lights popped one by one. A violent, unseasonal rain left puddles in the man's home office, where the Woman had put up curtains and shelves; the water shorted out his computer and warped the wood on the shelves.

The man could feel a charged heaviness descend upon his house, like the static in the air just before a thunderstorm.

THE DAY THE Gyutou learned its highest purpose, Samantha had been rudely awakened by a spring that had uncoiled from deep within the bowels of the mattress. It had poked her viciously in her left side, as she slept in the space where the Woman once lay.

The spring's attack was the most ferocious so far in an escalating mutiny of objects. The metal coil had poked a tiny hole just under Samantha's left breast that was now bleeding slightly. She cursed and swore, then ran out to the kitchen to get a hammer, a pair of pliers, anything to beat the spring back into retreat.

She chanced upon the Gyutou first; it immediately sensed her rage, crackling in the air of the kitchen. As she reached out for the knife, its blade nicked her forefinger and she howled in anger. *Damn you,* she said, grabbing it by the handle. She raced back into the bedroom and tried to use the blade as a lever to force the spring back into the mattress. But the coil sprang back violently again; and this time, as though carried along by a rising force, the Gyutou slipped and cut deep into the palm of her right hand.

Furious now, Samantha tried to make her way to the kitchen to cleanse her wounds, getting ready to fling the knife into the garbage bin.

But the Gyutou was not the only thing in the apartment cursed with longing for the Woman. A small wool rug that she had plucked from a sale rack at the textile store rebelled against Samantha's feet, which had time and again ground dirt viciously into its hair. At this moment, it summoned all its anger, raising its hackles so that she tripped on it and was thrown completely off balance. Arms flailing, she knocked a heavy cast-iron skillet that the Woman had used to make many of the man's meals off its perch on the metal shelf above the stove. It sighed the Woman's name in the wind as it fell on Samantha's head, cracking her skull.

Screaming, she tried to brace herself against the washing machine, and this caused it to begin tilting.

She dropped the knife on the tiled floor. And as her body fell, the Gyutou rose to meet her. It felt the young woman's weight on the tip of its blade for the merest fraction of a second, before its still-sharp blade entered her chest and buried itself in her heart.

It was as the Gyutou had suspected all along: Samantha's

blood sang only of herself, of her own desires and needs and cravings, her shallowness and greed, her meanness and malice. There was no hint of sacrifice or selflessness in her blood-song, no suffering except the denial of her wants.

And the Gyutou became even more enraged that her blood-song bore the notes of another's suffering: the Woman's.

This was what the Gyutou had been waiting for: the moment that a knife like it learned its highest Purpose.

With terrible clarity, it finally knew that it had been made, not for not love, but for vengeance.

At this same moment, the washing machine fell like a tree in a forest. The machine, to which the Woman had entrusted her clothes and those of her faithless beloved, and the linens of the bed they shared, came crashing down on Samantha's neck and head. It crushed vertebrae and skull, finishing the job the bed spring had started.

Even as consciousness and life drained from her, Samantha thought only of herself: she wondered if all this would have happened if they had thrown out all of the Woman's things sooner.

WHEN THE MAN arrived home later that night, he knew instinctively that something had gone terribly wrong. She didn't come to the door, didn't answer when he called her name. As he entered the tiny flat, he saw a thin trail of blood leading from the bedroom door. Just beyond the threshold of the kitchen, he saw Samantha's bare feet, now pale against the gray tile.

He pushed aside the washing machine to get to the young woman and was horrified at the slick blood that had pooled beneath her. He turned her over so that she lay on her side, and then he saw the Gyutou sticking out of her chest. Without thinking, he grasped the knife's handle, pulling the blade out.

It was not long before he heard footsteps at the door of the apartment. One of the neighbors had heard the commotion and telephoned the police.

The Gyutou was satisfied. Its blade, its soul, would forever bear the name of the Woman. But now its handle bore the mark—the fingerprints—of the man.

In the city's biggest jail, hidden inside a thin, filthy mattress, a weapon fashioned from a hammered tin can and a length of electrical tape felt a familiar stirring.

PROMISES TO KEEP

She knew it would be cold in Europe this time of year. But when she stepped out of the rental car, the skin on her face felt as though it had been drawn tight over the bone. She shut the car door firmly and pocketed the keys. She hugged herself to keep warm, tucking her gloved hands underneath her armpits, ruing the thinness of her coat.

The canal across the street was still, the water like gunmetal beneath a winter sky. *Six meters deep*, he had told her many years before, *so easy to just drive into it and let it take you.*

The street was quiet and empty, just as he said it would be at this hour. She looked up and down it, once, twice. He did not have many neighbors. The young people would be at work; the old people would be puttering around in their homes or backyards.

The gate was unlocked, and she let herself in easily and quickly. She could hear chickens clucking from the back of the main house. She started walking up the path to the house, then paused midway, listening for other sounds. A moment later, satisfied that there was no one else around, she went on. The front door, too, was unlocked.

She was surprised at how familiar it all seemed, even though she had never been here before. There was the lamp he bought while on assignment in Manila, where they first met. There were the two large dog beds that his German shepherds hardly ever used because they preferred to sleep at the foot of his bed. Both dogs had to be re-homed after he became too ill to care for them. Not long after that, he had become too ill to care for himself.

She realized that she knew the layout of the house almost as well as she did her own. He had taken her on a guided tour of the house before, via his phone camera: him still strong, still mobile, chatting away as though she were right there with him. She even remembered—how, she could not fathom—the quality of light as it filtered in, wan and cold, through the windows. The layout could be easily explained. The light was another thing altogether, something not easily discernible from a webcam's jumpy, grainy pictures.

She was careful not to touch anything unless it was absolutely necessary, even though she had kept her gloves on. She walked up the stairs, the wood creaking softly beneath her feet. Second floor, last door on the right. As she came closer, she recognized hospital smells, disinfectant and bleached floors and alcohol. She pushed the door open.

There was a wooden chair beside his bed, and she knew it had last been occupied by the day nurse. A few books on the bedside table—the nurse read to him for an hour every morning, and then she would leave to go shopping for the day's meals, not that he ate much anymore. She would be away for at least two hours because she biked to the center of town, and she liked to while away some time chatting with friends in between errands. Just enough time to do what had to be done.

She sat down in the chair. The seat was still warm. She could not help but marvel at their timing, his and hers. He had always been a meticulous planner. And she had always been good at following instructions.

THREE MONTHS. THAT'S all the time they had spent together, all those years ago. He had come to Manila to work on a project for his company; she had just moved back from a three-year job rotation in Singapore a few months before, feeling lost and alienated from the city of her birth. They had met at an art gallery, literally stumbling upon each other in a darkened exhibit hall. He had asked her, then and there, to have coffee with him. Coffee became dinner, a movie, a walk to his hotel. They spent nearly every night together after that, but for only three months.

So little time, when she thought about it. But just enough to let him into her life, to learn about his, to get used to his presence: the sound of his voice, the feel of his hands on her body, the texture of his skin, his warmth in the bed beside her, his smell.

His smell. She could never pinpoint exactly what it was. Most of the time he smelled like the freshest laundry, and sometimes a note of aftershave or toothpaste. The slightest hint of pungency when he exerted himself while making love, but always, always underscored by the scent of warm, clean skin, like the top of a baby's soft, bald head. It was strongest when she buried her face in the center of his chest, or pressed her nose to the nape of his neck, that precious unnamed space beneath ear and hairline. She remembered thinking that if she could smell this scent for the rest of her life, she would be completely happy.

But she couldn't. He loved her in his own way, as she loved him, but he could not stay. His work took him all over the world, and save for the time they had spent together, he lived without attachments. He was simply not the kind of man who married, made babies, grew old and toothless surrounded by children and grandchildren. And she knew that she was the kind of woman who did.

A few nights before they were to say goodbye, she found herself crying in bed. He touched her face but she begged him, *don't. Don't be so nice to me.* When she struggled to get out of bed, so he would not see her tears, he held her tighter. *You're not going anywhere.*

She had asked him, *How do I go back? Back to work, every day, seeing the same people, then back home. Make dinner. Watch television. Go to bed, fall asleep without you beside me. Lather, rinse, repeat.*

He didn't have any answers. He just said, *I wish I could slow the time until I have to leave.*

SHE HAD NOT really looked at him until this moment, and what she saw made her want to weep. His body under the blanket was skeletal—*now, don't be shocked, Vivienne, it will look really bad but that's just how it is.* How many times, a lifetime ago, had she seen that body, touched it, reveled in it, been enveloped and pleasured and fascinated by it? His face, gouged with deep lines by the pain radiating from his bones and spine. His hair, once dark, now a fine white fuzz on his scalp. An IV drip inserted in a bony hand.

He began to stir, and she sat motionless, not wanting to startle him. When he opened his eyes, he did not seem to see her. A moment or two later, he could see her but did not seem to recognize her.

"Hey," she said quietly.

Then he knew it was her, and he smiled. "Hey. You're here."

"You say 'Jump,' I say, 'How high?'"

"Bit early in the day for a Debbie Gibson reference, isn't it?"

"I was thinking Cheap Trick, but hey, whatever floats your boat."

He chuckled, then looked at her as though he were laying the memory of her face from eleven years ago over the face he was seeing now, lining up each curve and angle and feature. "I'm so glad you came." He held out a hand, thin and veined against the white sheet. She removed the glove from her right hand and took his very, very gently, remembering warnings that his nerve endings would be particularly sensitive.

"Well, you've always had a way of compelling me to do things against my better judgment."

"I'm sorry."

"What are you sorry for? I said they were against my better judgment. I didn't say I didn't want to do them."

He wrinkled his nose. "What's the difference?"

She sighed, pretending exasperation. "You remember

you once asked me about skydiving in Cebu or Zambales? You seemed so interested in it, and I asked if you were serious. You said you'd probably throw up, but it was something you had to try at least once in your life. Even against your own better judgment."

He shook his head in disbelief. "I said that?"

"Uh-huh."

"I was a twat."

She raised an eyebrow. "*Was?*"

They both laughed, but soon he was wincing, and the wince turned into a coiled, tortured writhing that he fought hard to control. The pain distorted his face, curled his lips into a grimace. She moved to help him, arms outstretched. But he waved her away, a gesture that told her what she already knew in her mind but not in the impulses of her body, that there was no help, not from her, not from doctors, not from drugs, not from some real or imagined God. She waited, hardly breathing, watched his legs twist under the sheets, his back arch, his elbows dig into the mattress. He made a sound that she had heard from neither human nor animal before, starting low in his throat, sliding up into a high-pitched mewl, ending in an almost inaudible whimper. Sweat beaded on his brow and his upper lip, and the fine, short hairs on his head matted together.

She waited until his limbs relaxed, until his breathing became more regular. She tried not to look as horrified. When the figure in the bed was finally still, she asked, in as even a voice as she could muster: "Shall I get you some water?"

His eyes were closed, but he held out his hand again, and she took it.

"Right here," he whispered, squeezing her hand. "This is all the water I need."

SHE TOOK HIM out to lunch, the day he was to fly back to his real life, to the farm by the canal, the daily commute to his workplace by bike and ferry, the months on assignment in far corners of the world. Back to his two German shepherds and half a dozen chickens.

"Do they lay eggs?"

"Not a one."

"And of course you can't cook them. Not if you've already named them."

On the surface, they both seemed carelessly happy, two people who would see each other again later that night, or tomorrow, or the next week, and many times again after that.

After lunch they went shopping—it was January, and the weather back home would be cold and wet and miserable. He bought a windbreaker. She, in a simultaneous burst of emotion and practicality, bought him a gray baseball cap to keep the rain off his head.

When the shopping was done, he seemed to indicate that they should part ways outside the mall. "I'm not going to say goodbye to you at a goddamned taxi stand," she said, quietly but firmly. He did not protest.

It was raining so they took a cab back to his hotel. He reached for her hand and snaked his fingers through hers.

Her heart seemed altogether too large and too heavy for her body, and she found it hard to breathe.

Once inside the room, he tried on the jacket and the cap, then turned to her for her opinion.

"Snazzy," she said.

"You think so?" he asked, smiling. "I don't look like a prick?"

She held her arms open and he walked right into them, then folded her into his own. They stood like that for a while.

"Miss me a little?" she asked, her voice muffled because her face was pressed to his chest.

"Oh yeah." He chuckled. "I'll miss you. Just a little, like an annoying pebble that's stuck in my shoe."

"Prick."

She maintained her composure after she left the room. And when she got into a cab that took her home. And when he boarded the plane that took him far away from her. She kept it together until days later, when, cleaning out the odds and ends that had accumulated in her wallet, she found the bill for that last lunch together. She was glad she found it while she was at home. How odd it would seem to strangers, after all: a woman sobbing over a restaurant receipt.

HE CAUGHT HER glancing at the clock on the bedside table. "We have plenty of time."

She reached out for the clock and adjusted the knob so that the minute hand moved forward slightly. "We had plenty of things, but time was never one of them." She set the clock back on the table.

"That's my fault."

"It's nobody's fault. That's just the way things were. Like you said, good jobs don't grow on trees. Besides, we couldn't give each other what we needed. So we gave each other what we could."

"And that was good enough for you?" He searched her face.

"I'm here now, aren't I?"

He stroked the palm of her hand. "I'm so very sorry."

SHE NEVER RETURNED to that restaurant, nor to any other restaurant where they had been together. She went to any other museum as long as it was not the same museum where they met. She declined invitations to events that took place in the hotel where they spent so many nights together. She held on to ticket stubs, museum flyers, receipts from those three months, put them in an envelope, hid them away in the bottom tray of her jewelry box.

They stayed in touch through the years, through his constant travels and occasional affairs, through her eventual marriage and motherhood. They remained each other's best-kept secret. But they agreed never to see each other again, even though he still came to Manila for work occasionally. He said, and she believed him, that he did not love anyone else; that part of him would always be in her keeping. He jokingly chided her for abandoning him for a husband and children, a normal life.

"And here I was, hoping that you'd die alone and miserable like me!"

"I don't care about you *that* much," she said.

"Well, how much do you care about me then?"

"I guess you'll find out someday."

SHE KNEW HE was ill, but for months she did not know how serious it was. He did not talk much about it and did not seem to appreciate being pressed for details. At some point he stopped using the camera on his phone, saying it had developed a defect. He kept putting off getting a replacement. The emails had dwindled to a trickle before stopping completely.

When the email came last month, she was stunned. She tried to call him, but he was apparently in and out of hospitals.

"He sleeps a lot," the private nurse who picked up the phone one day told her.

"Does he ever get on the computer?"

"Sometimes, if he feels strong enough."

The nurse didn't want to say anything else, so she asked: "Look, I know you don't know me and you can't say very much. So I'll ask you a question, and if you don't say anything, that means yes. Is he in pain?" Silence. "Is it bad?" More silence.

She started asking doctors, and friends and relatives who were doctors, and friends and relatives who knew doctors, *what is this thing, how bad is it, what can be done*.

And they all said the same thing, *it's very bad, and it will* get worse. It will be torture and it will be god-awfully slow. He will lose everything bit by painful bit. There's nothing to be done, except to manage it, and at some point, when it can no longer be managed, he will be trapped in a body that has become a cage of pain.

One day she was finally able to get him on the phone. He sounded like himself, albeit a little hoarse. The nurse had whispered to her that he was having a rare good day, before handing him the receiver. He waited until the nurse left the room before speaking.

It was during that conversation that he asked her to come to him.

Her first response was *no, I can't. You don't know what you're asking me.*

"I do. That's why I asked you to think about it."

"I have a husband, a family." At first, she tried to be kind, but then she was furious, and the words came spilling out, all the hurt and resentment of the years lived without him. "You always were a selfish bastard. Why would I want to do this for you? You left. Do you have any idea how long it took to pick up the pieces and glue myself back together again? And now you have the gall to ask this of me. You get away scot-free and guess who's left holding the bag again."

He didn't interrupt, just let her talk, let her say everything she'd been holding on to all these years. When he finally spoke, he sounded sad but resigned.

"I know, Viv," he said quietly. "It's a lot to ask. And I understand if you can't. I just thought . . . I thought it would be really nice to see you again, at last."

• • •

BUT SHE CAME to a decision, and she stuck with it. They made plans, like they used to another lifetime ago, finalizing dates, making travel arrangements, getting the logistics down pat. He insisted that they discuss things over the phone—no emails, no letters, no chats over the internet. A part of her—the part that was still wild, still reckless, with no husband to make dinner for and no kids to raise—came to life again. She found herself looking in the mirror one day, wondering if he would still find her attractive after more than a decade, if the lines and wrinkles in her face would betray her age and her cares, if he would mind the weight she had gained after three pregnancies.

When she caught herself thinking these thoughts, she reminded herself that she was married to a good man: a man who had not swept her off her feet, who did not set her heart racing madly, but who had won her with his quiet devotion, and then kept her with a calm, clear-eyed, loving steadiness.

When her husband came home from work one afternoon, not too long after that first phone call, she sat him down. She took in his short, stocky frame, his round face and glasses—the solid, completely-there-ness of him—and with a deep breath, she started telling him about the man who lived on a farm in a faraway country. She told him there was something she needed to settle with that man, and that it was best that he didn't ask too many questions. She asked him to trust her, but above all, to forgive her, for that bit of herself that she could never give him because it belonged to someone else.

He was quiet for a while, and his face was stony. He didn't look at her. Then he stood up and walked away. He left the house and didn't come back until the early hours of the next morning. He avoided her for several days after that, speaking only to the children. On weekdays, he stayed late at work; on weekends, he locked himself up in his home office and did not come out, even for meals.

When he'd decided to break his long silence, he asked: "Whatever it is—would you regret not doing this more than you would doing it?"

She thought about it, and then gave him her answer.

"All right, then," he said, and stood up, fishing his car keys out of a pocket in his trousers. "You'll need some warm clothes."

HE WATCHED HER. "Your return all sorted out?"

"Yes," she said. She had spent a few days sight-seeing in the country before coming here. After this, she would drive to France, a journey of several hours, with stops along the way. She would spend a few days in Paris, avoiding places where she might bump into friends or relatives, and fly back to Manila from there. Just an ordinary tourist traveling through Europe for a week or so. Nobody would even know that she had stopped at the farm. He seemed satisfied.

"I just want to be sure, you know. That this is what you want."

He looked at her with a sad hope in his eyes. "It's the only option left to me. They allow it here, but only under very strict conditions, and I don't fit into every one of them as required by law. And there's no one to advocate for me. The alternative is too . . ." and here his voice faltered. "Honestly, Viv, I don't want to know what that will be like."

She stood up and settled into the bed beside him. His body was so very frail now, she was afraid she might crush him. She put her arms around him, cradled his head against her chest. He still smelled the same—that wonderful, clean-laundry, warm-skin scent—but underneath it now was a trace of something she did not recognize and could not name, something old and heavy and bitter. It did not matter; she inhaled deeply, again and yet again, and soon she was no longer afraid.

"Let's do this."

He looked up at her like a child, relief, gratitude, remorse, sadness in his face. He pointed to a bookshelf on the other side of the room. "Brown paper package tied up with string."

She eased herself out of his arms and out of the bed, slipped the glove back on to her right hand and went over to the bookshelf, found the package in seconds.

"Should I ask how you got it?"

He shook his head: no.

She returned to his bedside and tore the wrapping paper open. A cardboard box, and inside, another box made of Styrofoam. And inside that box, a syringe and a vial filled with liquid.

He was there to guide her along, but she worked quickly, having memorized his instructions by heart. It would have gone faster without the gloves on, but she had to be careful not to leave any prints.

When it was done, there was nothing to do but wait. She slid into bed beside him again, and he nestled in her arms. They lay together like that for what seemed like a very long time. They didn't speak, and there really wasn't anything else to be said.

And then it was over, and it was time to go. She laid him back on the pillows gently, smoothed his hair as she had done so many times before with her children. She arranged his arms and legs so that they would not be twisted stiff later. She pulled the blanket up to his chest, but not so neatly that it would look like someone else had done it for him.

He looked like he was merely asleep. He had told her it would seem as though his heart had failed; it was not very common in people with this disease, but not so uncommon that experts would look too closely. Even if they did, she would be long gone by then. This is what it all came down to: why he had asked her to come. Why he had planned every detail—from the time she would arrive to how long she would stay, to ensuring that she knew exactly what she was doing. Why he did not put anything in writing. Why it had to be her.

She checked the clock on the bedside table. The nurse would be back soon.

He had instructed her to look inside the drawer in the table. When she opened it, she found a worn, faded baseball cap. She took it and clutched it to her chest. He, too, had held on to things.

She kissed him one last time, on the forehead. Then she put the cap in one coat pocket, the vial and syringe in the empty box along with the gloves. She tucked the box under her arm and walked out of the room, out of the house, out of the gate.

She got into the car and pulled out onto the street. The sky had cleared up a little; the water in the canal was calm. She had not driven far when she saw a woman on a bicycle coming in the opposite direction. The bike's basket was full: some vegetables, a jug of milk, a loaf of bread, a magazine.

Vivienne looked straight ahead. She did not glance at the woman when she passed her, nor check the rearview mirror as she pedaled toward the gate of his farm.

There was a long journey ahead. She kept driving.

HARVEST

They're very easy, white men. They come to this part of the world in their suits and ties and expensive shoes, rushing through airports and hotel lobbies with their briefcases and laptops, swollen with a sense of their own importance. But really, they're like children, ruled by their wants, enslaved by their appetites. They do not see how easy they are to read.

Take this man, for example, lying in bed with his pants around his ankles. He didn't bother to take his socks off; he was in too much of a hurry to get to the good part. Dark fur on his chest, fuzz on his arms and legs, a patch on the back of his head where his dark brown hair is starting to thin. But he's still relatively young, with a good physique, a nonsmoker who exercises regularly. Lee and Joel, they're good at choosing marks; they do all the spadework necessary. My job is just to reel them in.

When we met at a bar earlier this evening, I pretended that I was intrigued, but cautious. I checked his right hand for a ring and made sure he noticed. He wasn't wearing it, but it was easy to see that he regularly wore one. A good sign; he'll think carefully about consequences when the time comes.

He tried to tell me what he was doing here but held just

enough back so that it would seem as though he were privy to matters too delicate and too important to be discussed with a stranger. I allowed him to think that I was impressed. I allowed the skirt of my wrap dress to slide off one thigh just so. I allowed him to gently touch my skin there.

Still, I behaved as though I was nervous and a little scared. I glanced around the bar every once in a while, as though I were anxious about being spotted by someone I knew. It was too early in the evening, the place wasn't crowded yet, just a few locals. The bar staff were busy chatting among themselves.

He took my hand, stroked the inside of my wrist, tracing with his thumb the vein there, went into the usual spiel, variations of which I now know by heart. *Are you afraid of me? Are you worried you'll be recognized?*

Are you thinking of someone else? Are you afraid of hurting him? We're not doing anything wrong. Life is short.

I think we have a real connection here. I don't want to look back on this moment and regret that I didn't do anything about it. Do you? You're so beautiful.

So transparent. So predictable.

Now here he is, lying where his appetites have led him. A nondescript hotel in the business district, with a Hispanic-sounding name implying class and sophistication. Nice enough to have a star or two, good air conditioning, and a working bathtub. But not nice enough to have top-notch security, or cameras installed at every corner.

There is a part of me that thinks he deserves what happens next, although I know he does not.

I look at my watch. Anita should be here soon. And I know that Lee and Joel will be late; that's just the way it is. On his own, Lee would probably be here on time. But none of us would be here on our own. Joel is the glue that holds us together. Joel is the trap we have all fallen into, the chain that binds us.

The first time I did this, I was sick for weeks afterward. But Joel was persuasive. He said we weren't exploiting our own people, weren't doing it to children, or the very poor. He made it sound like we were somehow an *ethical* operation, targeting only those who could very well afford to lose what we took from them. As Joel always told us, some very rich people wanted what only we could give them, and they were willing to pony up big time for it. He never gave us names, but sometimes Lee would show Anita and me a newspaper story or send us a link to a website, and leave us to reach our own conclusions.

In the end, though, the money was better than anything I could make as a sales rep or a secretary or a call center agent. So I turned up for a second time, and a third, not that I had a choice. Not that any of us did, because Joel's friends in high places had friends in low places—the places where we lived and walked and shopped and ate every day. The places where we could be watched and followed, and, if necessary, brought back into line.

After a while I just went dully along. And as long as I didn't have to be in the bathroom when the thing happened, I could fool myself into thinking that I wasn't actually a part of it.

• • •

WHILE I WAIT, I prepare. I snap on a pair of gloves. I run a bath and turn off the tap when the tub is about a third of the way full. I remove the pillows and strip the sheets off the bed. To do this, I have to roll him several times from side to side. He doesn't wake. I take the pillows, roll the sheets into a bundle, toss them into the closet.

There is a knock on the door, and by the rhythm—*tap-tappa-tap-tap*—I know it's Anita. I open the door. She's wearing a chambermaid's uniform, and she has one of the hotel's service trolleys.

Anita is in her midfifties, a stocky, hard-looking woman. Or perhaps this business is making her look hard, making all of us look hard. I don't know. Very early on, I learned not to ask questions. I don't know anybody else's story, not Lee's, not Anita's, certainly not Joel's. The only story I know is my own, and it is my hard luck that Joel knows it too. Joel knows all our stories. Otherwise, we would not be here.

Anita moves briskly, efficiently, looking down both sides of the hallway to make sure nobody is watching. She puts a stack of neatly folded plastic sheeting in my arms, and then takes two massive bags of tube ice from within the bowels of the trolley.

"You run the bath yet?" she asks.

I nod.

I can sense her impatience as she brushes past me. For

some reason, Anita has decided that she doesn't like me. I'm not sure why, although I don't suppose I blame her.

I lock the door, go back inside, and stand by the bathroom door to see if she needs anything. When she looks up and sees me, the irritation flares up and spreads across her face like a fast-blooming rash.

"What are you waiting for? Start laying those down!" she says, gesturing toward the sheeting in my arms.

I sigh, turn, and do what she says. The sheeting is thin but durable, and one piece is enough to cover the entire bed. I roll the man around again to get the sheeting underneath him. Anita emerges from the bathroom, surveys my efforts for a moment. I'm out of breath from moving him around but she makes no attempt to help me. With a grunt, she turns away and goes back to the trolley for more ice.

As I start laying down the sheeting on the floor, I hear her come back into the room. I ignore her, she ignores me. She disappears into the bathroom again, and soon I hear the ice tumble into the bathtub.

A few minutes later, it is her turn to stand at the bathroom door, looking at me on my hands and knees laying down the plastic. I look at her.

"All set in there?" I ask.

"Mm-hmm."

"Good," I say, for lack of anything else.

Again, she does not try to help me.

"How old are you?" she asks suddenly.

"What?"

"How old. Are you." She says it slowly, as though she is talking to someone slow.

"Thirty-four," I say, as I lay the last of the sheets down.

"That's not young."

"Thanks."

"I mean, you look younger. Young enough to be stupid."

"Thanks, Anita. So many compliments today."

She draws in a quick, deep breath. "What I mean is—if you were younger, I'd understand. Young people can be stupid."

"Old people can be stupid, too," I say, spotting an opening. "You're what? Fifty, sixty?"

She smiles, but it's a sad smile. "I *am* stupid. Never made it past grade school. Never done anything with my life but clean up after other people. They throw up, they piss, they crap, and I clean it all up. The one time I try to be smart, the one time I try to get ahead—"

She falls silent a moment, then she fixes me in a hard stare. "But you. Look at you. You're educated, you're pretty. You seem like a sensible girl. You got parents?"

"Everyone's got parents."

"You know what I mean. Parents who were around for you. Put you through school. Taught you what's what."

This one stings worse than anything. I think about my father and my mother, him gone ten years, her gone just after this whole business started. When I lie to myself, I say that she's the real reason why I'm still here—to pay off the hospital bills, and the credit card debts, and the loans from government agencies and relatives and friends.

She isn't. Anita is right, I *am* stupid. *I* am the real reason I'm here. Desperate and lonely, I fell for a snake and soon found it impossible to extract myself from its jaws.

"My parents are dead," I say quietly.

She considers this a moment. "They're probably better off that way." Although the words are tough as usual, this time they don't come out that way. "Lee says you have a kid."

I nod. "Six years old."

"The father?"

"He left when I got pregnant and never looked back."

She snorts with a contempt that for once does not seem to be directed at me. "That's what they do. No surprises there." She looks around the room, then at the man on the bed. "I guess you're all set." Her voice softens again, for only the second time since I've known her. "You going to be okay?"

How do I even answer that? "Yes."

She nods, heads for the door. "Tell Joel I'll be back with more ice later. And I'll clean up when you're all done. Like always."

She steps out into the corridor, looks both ways. Then without another word, she wheels the trolley down to the elevators.

I lock the door. I sit on the chair at the dressing table, where I can see the sleeping man in the mirror. I wait.

FINALLY, THERE IS a knock on the door and I rush to answer it.

"It's about time," I hiss.

Joel stands big and tall in the doorway, smoking, grinning. I snatch the cigarette from between his lips and stub it out on the hard wood of the doorframe, at a spot where nobody would think to look. He smiles even wider, swaggers through the door and into the room, which now feels very small and airless.

Lee follows close behind him. He looks at me, and then at the cigarette butt.

"He shouldn't be smoking in here," I say through my teeth.

Lee is a small, quiet, serious man, the one who really knows what needs to be done in that bathroom, and how to do it. I doubt that he wants to be here any more than I do. "You don't want to leave that in here," he says softly. "Put it in your pocket."

I do what he says and move aside to let him pass. He's struggling with heavy black bags and wheeled suitcases. Inside them are the things we'll be using—portable monitors, surgical instruments, bottles of saline solution, packs of plasma. As usual, Joel has not offered to help.

"Cooler's in the hallway by the door," he calls out over his shoulder. I nod, rush back out of the room and pick up the blue rubber cooler.

Suddenly a door opens, and a middle-aged white man emerges from one of the rooms. He glances in my direction, obviously likes what he sees, gives me a smile. "Looks like you're having a picnic," he says, pleasantly.

"A what?" I'm momentarily confused. He gestures toward the cooler, and I understand. "Oh, this. I–"

"Honey?" Joel's voice floats into the hallway from inside the room, and there is a note of warning in it that I'm certain only I can hear. "You want to bring those beers in?"

"Sure, baby." I pick up the cooler, register the regret that flickers across the man's face.

"Good evening, miss," he says, then turns away and walks in the direction of the elevators.

I want to run after him. I want to beg for his help, to tell him what's going on. What we're about to do to another man, a stranger just like him, passing through on business, lonely for company. I want to tell him, *look, the next time it could be you. So please. Help me.*

But I feel a hand close over my throat and I'm pulled roughly back into the room, shoved up against a wall as the door closes. I feel Joel's warm body pressing hard against my back, his stubble against my skin, his lips against my ear.

"You thinking of trying anything funny, sweetheart?" When I don't answer, his fingers tighten over my throat. "Sweetheart?" he repeats.

"No. No, of course not, Joel."

"You sure, babe?" His voice is a caress, cool silk draped over a sharp blade. "Our client is paying us a lot of money for this one. More than double what we made the last time. And the stakes are pretty high, with the elections coming up." His breath is hot on my neck. "Hope you're not planning to cause any trouble for us."

Lee clears his throat, and then calls out to us from the side of the bed where he stands, staring at the unconscious man. "This guy's going to wake up soon if we don't get moving."

Joel relaxes his grip. "Don't forget, sweetheart. I know where your little girl goes to school."

I touch my neck with trembling fingers. "No, Joel," I say, in a voice as calm and even as I can make it. "I won't forget."

He turns away, strides back into the room, spreads his arms wide and beams at Lee. "Okay, man. Let's get this party started."

I take a moment to compose myself, to steady the cold that has crept up my spine, the weakness in my knees.

Then, without really thinking, I take the cigarette butt from my pocket and drop it on the carpet, a tight spot in between the wall and a side table. I push it in with my toe, deep into the thick pile, where I know Anita can't find it. Maybe someone else will. Someone who's actually looking for it.

Maybe they won't find it this time. So I'll do it the next time, and the next.

Our luck has to run out sometime.

ORIGINAL SIN

The ride from the airport to Quezon City feels like an eternity, cars everywhere, sidewalks choked with people. It's so much hotter in Metro Manila now than it used to be when I was growing up. I felt it as soon as I stepped out of the terminal to look for a cab, slamming headlong into that wall of heat and humidity. Maybe it's global warming; maybe it's the thirteen million or so people crammed into an area of 620 square kilometers. So many lured to this sprawling, chaotic metropolis by the promise of economic opportunity, only to be let down by the reality that this promise is reserved only for a select few. The rest have to fight and steal and grift and hustle for scraps.

Like this cab driver. When I got into the cab at NAIA, I'd fully expected him to try and squeeze me for extra money. And so he does—another two hundred pesos when I arrive at the house in Fairview, with a well-practiced routine about how he needs to make the long trip through heavy traffic worth his while. Whatever. I'm too tired from the flight to argue.

He drives away and I walk up to the gate, ring the doorbell once, twice. A minute or two, then I ring again. The yellow bells have become unruly, their stems gone woody from a lack of pruning. The grass grows thick around the flat, irregular stone steps leading from the gate through the lawn to the front door. The house itself still looks good, though, with its white walls and its placa romana roof.

The screen door swings open. She hasn't changed much. She's wearing her hair very short now, like Jean Seberg in *Breathless*. It's perfect with her unusual face, her high cheekbones and full lips and dark eyes. She's squinting because she isn't wearing her glasses and can't see me very well through the gate. Those long fingers, so accomplished at Debussy and Bach and Liszt on the piano, never learned how to handle contact lenses, so she stopped trying years ago.

She walks slowly, hesitantly, toward the gate. When she recognizes me, she stops halfway across the lawn, all pale skin and white cotton housedress against the green.

"Greg?" She shakes her head in disbelief. "It can't be you."

"And yet it is." Still she stands and stares, her eyes wide in alarm, the color drained from her already pale face. "Come on, Grace, it's too hot out here. Let me inside already."

She starts, as if roused from sleep, rushes to let me into the yard. She closes the gate, then turns to me, wringing her fingers, her small, white teeth biting her lower lip.

"Hey." I put a hand under her elbow.

She pulls away. "You should have called first." She turns and walks right back into the house, leaving me in the burning sun.

• • •

I WAKE UP at four in the afternoon; I've been doing this for several days now. Today is Sunday. I can hear her at the piano downstairs, playing sections of Granados's *Goyescas*. I close my eyes and listen, imagine her fingers on the keys, her beautiful neck bent just so. I resist the urge to sneak up on her, the way I used to all those years ago, to put my hands over her eyes and to have her stop playing, touch my hands lightly, pretend she can't guess who it is. I cannot do these things anymore.

I get up from the bed and go to the bathroom to take a quick shower. By the time I'm finished, the music has stopped. I get dressed, proceed downstairs, and see her lying on the sofa with her eyes closed. The heat is oppressive; she has an electric fan directed toward her.

"I'm hungry."

She opens her eyes and sits up. "What do you feel like having?"

"I'll go make myself a sandwich." I inspect the contents of the refrigerator: green beans on a Styrofoam plate, watermelon wedges covered with cling wrap, cold cuts in the chiller. I take out a package and call out so she can hear me in the living room. "Do I need to fry this paprika loaf thing?"

"No," she says in a quiet voice, as she takes the package from my hands. I'd almost forgotten that she hardly makes a sound when she walks. She goes to the counter, takes some bread from a covered basket, another trip to the refrigerator for lettuce and tomatoes and mayonnaise. Her hands are just as efficient making a sandwich as playing the piano; the movements are spare, but with a kind of poetry to them that I remember with my heart, the way a child remembers its mother's voice. "You haven't heard Mass," she observes.

"I'll live."

"There's a five P.M. Mass at the parish church. And then another one at seven P.M." She is silent for a moment, waiting, but I don't answer. With a sigh, she takes a serrated knife and cuts the sandwich in two diagonally. "Planning to stay long?"

I sit on one of the high stools at the counter and take half of the sandwich from the plate she is holding out. "Not if you keep trying to make me hear Mass."

She tries to hide her face, busying herself with clearing things away and cleaning up. "You had it good at that company you were working for. That investment bank. I can't remember the name."

"Oh, were you there? I didn't see you."

She ignores my sarcasm. "New York was good for you. You couldn't find a job like that here."

"Thank goodness. It almost killed me."

She puts the leftover lettuce back in the vegetable compartment and stands in front of the open refrigerator for a moment. "What will you do, then?"

"I don't know. But I'll think of something."

Another sigh, barely audible, and she decides to change the subject. "How's Leslie?" The woman I was once engaged to, and who at this very moment is probably cursing me for leaving her, sneaking out of our apartment like a thief in the night with just a few belongings so I could make it to my flight in time.

"She's fine."

"Does she know you're here?"

"Nope."

"Are you finished?"

"Nope." I hold up what's left of the sandwich and wave it at her.

"Not the sandwich, Greg. You and Leslie."

"Oh. Pretty much." I want to sound flippant because I know it annoys her. But I didn't make the decision to come back in haste. I'd thought about it for years, even when I didn't know I was thinking about it. I didn't accumulate stuff in all my years abroad, not books, not clothes, not even a rice cooker, so essential for the Asian living far from home. Maybe I always knew that I would have to make a quick, clean getaway someday.

She plants the heel of her right hand on her right temple, rubbing it in a small circular motion; it's clear that talking to me is giving her a headache. "I thought you were going to marry her." She moves away from the refrigerator to sit across from me at the counter, folds her hands neatly in her lap, and avoids my eyes.

"That makes two of us." I finish my sandwich and shake crumbs from my fingers onto the plate. "I came back for you."

"Don't say things like that." She is just about to jump off the stool, but I grasp her wrist. "Stop it. Let me go."

"That's not what you wanted to hear?"

"Go to hell."

"Someday."

"You told me you were leaving for good."

"Papa told you I was leaving for good. He told you it was God's will."

She winces at the mention of him and wrenches her hand free. "You never should have come back." She gets off the stool and runs out of the kitchen. My throat has suddenly gone dry.

MY PARENTS ARE both dead. They sent me away in anger, told me they were ashamed of me. I never saw them again. Mutually we put years and miles between us, clinging to the anger because in its own barbed and poisonous way it was comfortable, familiar; it steeled us against one another. When first Mama died, then Papa, the anger gradually lost its meaning, betraying me in its new impotence.

Still, I didn't come home, unwilling to face the rest of the family. Over the years, I would occasionally find myself showing some visiting cousin or busybody aunt around the city. Always, as we sat together at some open-air café in Little Italy, or on the benches at Battery Park waiting for the ferry to Liberty Island, or around the boating pool at Central Park, there would be an undercurrent of tension in our conversations, always this one question hanging in the air between us. They would circle carefully around the black hole of the past, tentatively probing its edges, itching to see what was inside.

I would sit there, listening, waiting, until they realized they would get no answers. Then they would start fidgeting, looking through handbags, rooting through pockets, checking their messages and emails, mumbling hasty goodbyes.

I COME HOME from a day of job hunting when a car pulls up to curb right outside our gate. I turn around and accidentally drop my house keys, and as I bend to pick them up, a male voice calls out to me. "Greg?"

I look up and have to force myself to smile when I recognize the face. "Alan. Been a long time."

"Hey, long time no see," he says, sticking his head out the car window. "You should have called and told us you were coming. We would have picked you up at the airport. When did you get back?"

"A few weeks ago. You still live around here?"

Alan is holding a cigarette in one hand. Flicking ash off the tip, he grins that smug, fatuous grin I remember so well: the first of my cousins to drive, first to get laid, first to smoke and drink and try drugs. "With the wife and three kids."

"Already? That's great." I can't help feeling sorry for the poor fool who married him. I unlock the gate and try to make a graceful exit. "Well, I've got to start dinner, so I'll see you around."

"Hey, how's Grace? I don't see her much anymore. She never visits."

I knew he'd bring her up sooner or later. "She's okay. Still teaching at UP."

"Yeah, I heard she had a concert at the CCP last month. Fine-looking woman, our Grace. It's a big shame she hides herself away in that house. It's not right. Not healthy." He is looking at me now as though he knows me, as though he can see beyond the surface all the way through to my secret sins.

"Hey, Alan, it's been nice catching up with you, but I have some work to do," I say. "I'll see you around, okay?"

He ignores my attempt to get rid of him. "Hey, listen, Greg. My youngest is having a birthday this weekend. Why don't you and Grace drop by? Cake and spaghetti for the kids and something extra for the grown-ups. You can meet the wife, and Mama and Papa will be glad to see you both."

No, they won't. "I'll have to ask Grace."

"I won't take no for an answer, okay? We're family. Come on, it'll be just like old times."

I slot a key in between each finger, as one might do when preparing to use them as a weapon. "I'll have to ask her."

"Sure, sure." He starts to drive away from the curb. "I'll be expecting you."

GRACE COMES HOME a little after seven. I've made dinner and set the table; she smells the scent of garlic and herbs in the air and looks at me in surprise. "I know how to cook," I say defensively; she probably remembers my first efforts in this very kitchen, which caused us to throw away half our pots and pans.

She smiles, and a look comes into her eyes for the briefest of moments, a look that makes me want to get closer to her. But she turns away, moving quickly to the living room to put her books, scores, and bags on a table.

I follow her there. "Alan dropped by."

Her head jerks up, and she drops a few books on the floor. "Alan?" she asks, bending at the waist as much to hide her face from me as to retrieve the books. "Whatever for?"

"Did you know he got married?"

She turns her back to me, pretending to put her books in order. "Of course."

"Well, his kid's having a birthday party."

"No." I should probably be surprised at the vehemence with which she says it, but I am not.

"I haven't even asked yet."

"Still no."

I reach for her, but she pulls away immediately, as though my touch carries the germs of some highly communicable disease. "Okay. You don't have to go if you don't want to."

Instinctively, she rubs the spot on her forearm that my fingers have just touched, the way one might rub a bruise or a slight burn. "I don't want to," she says through gritted teeth. "I don't want people staring at me. Talking about me."

"Nobody will stare at you," I say soothingly.

"I said no."

"Okay, relax." I reach for her again, wanting, not wanting, *damn it all, stand still.*

"Don't. Don't do that."

"I'm not doing anything."

"Yes, you are."

The doorbell rings, and she turns toward the front door anxiously. "God, who can that be? Nobody ever comes here."

"It's okay, I'll see who it is." I walk out of the house and to the gate. There's a woman and a little girl about three years old standing outside it. I've never seen either of them before.

"Good evening." The woman is small, with a pretty, friendly face, and the child looks just like her. "Greg? Greg Marcial?"

"Yes, that's me. Can I help you?"

"Hi, I'm Nina." She smiles brightly, even as I continue staring at her. "Alan's wife. Your cousin-in-law."

"Oh."

She waits patiently as I unlock the gate and step aside for her to enter. "Alan asked me to stop by and drop off an invitation to our daughter's birthday party." She hands me a small white envelope, then lifts the child up toward me. "And this is your niece, Angelica. The birthday girl."

"Happy birthday, birthday girl," I say.

Nina asks the child, "Do you have a kiss for Tito Greg?" Angelica hesitates a fraction of a second, then puts her arms around my neck and gives me a gentle kiss on the cheek. I cannot believe either of them is related to Alan.

The screen door creaks behind me, and when I turn, Grace is looking out tentatively. "Grace, this is Nina, Alan's wife." I give her a stern look, which I know Nina cannot see from where she's standing. If Grace is thinking of scurrying back into the house, that look is enough to make her change her mind. She walks slowly toward the three of us and strangely enough, the child runs toward her, barreling into her legs and hugging them tight around the knees. Grace is so astonished that she stands there motionless, not knowing what to do. "Hello. What's your name?"

"That's Angelica. Angel, this is Tita Grace."

"Tita Glaice," the child says, looking up at Grace as though she is a fairy princess.

"She's adorable," Grace says, a little overwhelmed. *What is she thinking*, I wonder; is she thinking about children she might never have, children who would have had her wide dark eyes, her slim build, her soft hair, her long, pale fingers?

Nina looks at her, and then at me, and I see no furtiveness, no suspicion or malice in her eyes. She is obviously unaware of the past, obviously did not grow up in this neighborhood, obviously has not been told anything by her husband. Not yet.

"Well, now you *really* have to come to her party. Saturday afternoon."

Grace smiles at the woman, the small, uncertain smile of someone unaccustomed to the kindness of strangers. "We'd love to. Thank you."

I'M WOKEN UP in the middle of the night by a noise from downstairs. I sit up; the night is hot, the air in the room almost velvety. My skin is damp, even though I'm wearing nothing but boxers. There it is again; the sound is coming from the kitchen. A slight twinge of fear; *did I lock the kitchen door properly?* I get up and pause at the door, catching a glimpse of myself in a small oval wall mirror, large dark eyes in a pale, angular face, before leaving my room. Grace's bedroom door is closed. I try not to make noise as I move down the stairs, across the living room.

The kitchen is dark, but there is a dull orange glow in one corner, and I know it is from the refrigerator light.

"Grace?"

She withdraws her head from the interior of the refrigerator. "Greg." I catch my breath; her body shows through her thin cotton nightdress, outlined in the orange light.

I can remember a time when she wasn't always so easily frightened or startled. I can remember when her laugh was easy, joyful, when she didn't dole out her smiles in small, tentative measures. Even now, now that she has become this pale, silent, withdrawn stranger, I can still remember everything about her that I loved. I can still remember a time when she loved me.

She closes the refrigerator door and draws the nightdress tighter about herself. "I just wanted some water."

"Okay."

We stand there, in the dark and the heat, and the words we do not say, the things we cannot speak of, hang cobwebby in the kitchen air between us. Then she walks past me and hurries upstairs to her room.

THE OLD TOYOTA will budge only for Grace; she puts a pink gift-wrapped package for Angel on my lap before we set off. She's nervous but in otherwise good spirits. It's a short drive to North Fairview. Alan lives with his family in the same compound where he and his brothers grew up. After fourteen years, I remember exactly where it is; we used to pass by it every day on the school bus as kids. His father was my father's brother; they were that branch of the family that could be counted on to say the most tactless things, to give the tackiest gifts, to be the most indiscreet about other relatives' trials and misfortunes. Unfortunately, they were also the most well-off; my father had made the mistake of turning to them for money all those years ago, to send me away. In my heart, I hope he regretted it till the day he died.

Nina meets us at the gate. There are children running around on the lawn; the party is in full swing. "I'm so glad you could come."

Grace allows Nina to kiss her on the cheek, but absently, because she is looking for the child. "Angel," Nina calls out. The child breaks away from a group of playmates and runs toward us. Grace's face lights up; she bends low, so the child can kiss her on the cheek.

"Well, well." Alan comes up to us, smiling broadly. His eyes are unnaturally bright, and his face is flushed; he has had more than a few beers already, and it is only a little after five o'clock. "Glad you could make it."

"Thanks for having us." I shake his hand, and he turns to Grace. She nods to him, then quickly turns away, busying herself with his child so that she doesn't have to talk to him. There is heaviness in my chest, a weight that has still to fall away after all these years, the sense of walking with eyes wide open into a burning house.

"This is the kids' territory," he tells me, gesturing toward the lawn, the swing and seesaw, the small people darting around them. "Come on inside."

There is a quiet elegance about the interior of the house that I cannot associate with Alan and his clan. I can only assume that the furnishings, the curtains, the beautifully patterned carpeting and the gray marble floor are reflections of Nina's more refined tastes. Once we walk into the living room, I feel a vague sense of dread; it is filled with familiar faces, childhood playmates, relatives. I see my uncle glaring at me from across the room, my aunt resolutely ignoring me. I glance at Grace. She looks at me imploringly, *this was not a good idea, let's go home.*

Nina takes her by the arm. "Come! There's grown-up food in here," she says cheerfully, oblivious to the sudden change in temperature in the room. Grace accepts the invitation gratefully, following her into the kitchen to get away from these people.

"Greg." Alan hands me a beer, slaps me on the back, and pulls me toward a corner where he and a few other men are drinking around a low circular table.

"Hey, Greg," one of the men says, "how long since you got back?" A bus mate from school, but I can't remember the name. I was always careful not to sit beside or behind him because he always smelled terrible; he still does.

"Almost a month."

"You must have made a killing in the States." It's

Alan's older brother Joey, bald and paunchy and reeking of beer.

"I wish."

For half an hour the beer flows, and the small talk, but suddenly Alan slaps my thigh with the back of his hand. "Hey, Greg, how about those American girls, huh?" His voice is louder than it needs to be, his speech slurring from all the beer he has consumed.

I know where this is going. I had known from the moment I saw him at the curb outside the house, from the moment he had given me that look, *I know you*, and yet I'd allowed myself to come here, to drag Grace along with me. God damn it, what was I thinking? That they would forget?

"Wasn't there a girl?" he continues. "What was her name?"

"Leslie."

"Leslie. That's it! Pretty, blond. Big—" and he cups both hands and brings them close to his chest. "Am I right? You know I'm right!" and everyone at the table roars with laughter.

"She's not in the picture anymore," I say quietly.

"Awww, that's too bad." He shakes his head. "That why you came home?" The innuendo provokes another round of laughter.

"I was exhausted from work. I needed a break. Too much stress."

"And maybe not enough—you know . . ." and he finishes the thought with another rude gesture that everyone gets, and there's howling and snorting all around, and they look like animals, with their red eyes and yellow teeth and beer breath. "Listen, Greg, who's Grace going out with? Anyone special?"

I put the beer down on the table and stare hard at it. "What Grace does with her life is her own business."

"Yeah, but who's going to take care of her? Know what I mean?"

"She's a big girl, she can take care of herself."

"It's a waste, if you ask me." Then he bursts out laughing. "But of course, now that you're back, you can both get some action."

My first instinct is to look around to see if anyone else has heard, and the first face I see is Grace's. Her eyes are wide, first with shock, then with shame. A glass tumbler falls from her hand and shatters into a hundred shards on the marble floor.

I grab my bottle of beer from the table. Everything is a blur; my hand moves ever so slowly as it throws the bottle at Alan's head. His face twists in pain. I hear a woman screaming, see people rising from their seats.

I turn and see Grace running out the door and I go after her. She stumbles once, twice, before getting to the gate. Someone tugs hard at my arm; it's Nina, furious. "What the hell, Greg, what is wrong with you?" she asks, over and over again. I shake her off.

Grace gets into the car and starts it. I run out the gate and try to stop her, but she steps on the gas and I have to jump out of the way. In seconds, the car disappears around the bend.

• • •

IT'S ALMOST MIDNIGHT. I haven't been able to sleep. Grace has locked herself in her room, and she won't talk to me. Now, in the darkness, her bedroom door creaks open, and she pads down the hall, coming this way. "Greg," she calls softly, rapping on the door.

I sit up. "Come in."

She opens the door. She doesn't come into the room, just stands in the doorway, watching me.

"What's wrong?" I ask, getting out of bed.

She leaves the door open. "You've been gone so long. I thought it would be different now." She is looking at me, in the dark, but it is as though she is not seeing me, not talking to me. "But nothing's changed," she says sadly, as though some disease that had been in remission for over a decade had come back to her with even greater force.

"Listen, about tonight," I start, but in the doorway behind her, I see two large, hard-shell suitcases. "You're going somewhere." It comes out as a statement, though I had meant it to be a question.

"Nothing's changed," she says again.

Beams of yellow light come through the window of my room and move slowly across the ceiling. Caught for a moment in the light, we are both reflected in the dresser mirror. And I am startled again, after all these years, by how much we look like each other, even though we're only fraternal twins.

Outside, the cab driver honks his horn. She turns, picks

up her bags, and walks away. And I know, when I hear the front door close, and the car door slam, and the sound of the engine as the cab drives away, that she's never coming back to this house, back to me, back to the things that have been buried all these years and should have stayed that way.

COMFORTER OF THE AFFLICTED

The neck is broken. That's why the head is turned at such an unnatural angle. The body is lying chest down on the floor, but the head tilts upward and twists sharply to the right, a rotation of more than ninety degrees. The eyes are open, staring. Her frozen expression makes Saenz think she did not go down meekly. Her fingernails are rimmed with foreign material from where she scratched her attacker, raked flesh, drew blood.

Senior Inspector Mike Rueda stands quietly behind the priest, waiting.

Saenz straightens up from a crouching position over the body with a slight groan.

"You okay, Father?" Rueda asks.

"I'm an old man," Saenz mumbles, almost to himself. He strips off the latex gloves, presses the heel of his left hand against his right eye. He is about to stuff the bloodstained gloves into the pocket of his jeans when Rueda reaches out to stop him.

For a man with a prizefighter's face, Rueda is surprisingly gentle. "Let me take those." He holds open his own gloved hand. Saenz realizes his mistake, grunts and hands the gloves over. He glances down at his jeans and notices a small red streak where the gloves have made contact with the denim.

"Like I said, Mike. An old man."

Rueda bags the gloves. "You need a vacation." He glances down at the woman's body. "Well, maybe after this one." He turns, motions for a young officer to take the small bag for disposal. When she's out of earshot, he moves closer to the priest. "So was it the broken neck, or the glass?"

She had fallen from the stairs onto a glass-top table. The blood that matted her hair came from a wound at the back of her head, where a broken table leg had embedded itself.

"Either, both," Saenz says. "What matters is, was she pushed?" He waves long fingers toward a section of the balustrade near the top that has given way. "You try a fracture-match on that, and I'm guessing the stress marks will be consistent with a forceful impact. Not with any mere weakness in either the structure or the material." Back to the woman, now, fully absorbed in her face. "Gave him hell, though. Her luck ran out at the top of the stairs, but before she went down, she made him suffer nearly much as she did."

Rueda surveys their surroundings. Books have fallen off shelves, picture frames been knocked off walls, furniture overturned. "Satisfied it's a *him*, then?"

Saenz nods. "There's a full-length mirror on the door of one of the bedrooms. It's cracked. Nothing lying around it, and a bit of blood and hair at the point of impact. So what cracked it was a someone, not a something. Someone's head, in fact."

"And it's a *him* because?"

"The hair is short." A note of exasperation lends a slight edge to his voice. "And the point of impact is a few inches above where it would have been, had that head been hers. She's, what—about fix-six, five-seven? Bit taller than the average for a woman here. So if the person who cracked the mirror is even taller, odds are that it's a man."

Rueda takes a deep breath, biting down his own frustration. Father Augusto Saenz is a forensic anthropologist by training, and technically his expertise wouldn't be needed for cases like this. But if Rueda and his people could see things as clearly, connect the dots as quickly as the Jesuit does, he wouldn't be asking him to his crime scenes so often. "Okay. I'll make sure someone gets samples from the mirror too."

Saenz doesn't answer, doesn't even seem to have heard. He is still looking intently into her face.

"You brave girl," he mutters. "You brave, brave girl."

HER PARENTS HAVE been arguing for what seems like hours but suddenly the shouting stops.

They told her to stay downstairs but she needs to know if it's all right to come up now, if they're going to start making dinner soon. So she creeps up the stairs and then she hears it, *thud-thud-thud* like someone hitting the wall with a fist, then gasping, panting, whispered words that she can't quite understand.

When she opens the door, her father has his hand around her mother's throat, and he is pounding her head against the headboard.

Blind instinct, blind rage, blind something else that the child can't understand makes her rush toward them, makes her clamber up the bed and onto his back. She grabs great thick fistfuls of his hair, tugs hard, and he releases his grip on her mother, pulls himself up from where he has been looming over the woman and pinning her down. He turns his attention to the screaming six-year-old on his back, and with one easy motion flings her off him.

The child falls and hits her head on the floor, pain blooming a dozen colors in her field of vision before bleeding into white, but she gets up and lunges for him, all fingernails and elbows and tiny sharp teeth. And he knocks her back just as easily as the first time, and still she comes back for more.

The fourth time she comes at him, he picks her up by an arm, shoves her out of the room and locks the door. The child doesn't know it yet, but her shoulder has been dislocated.

UNDER ORDINARY CIRCUMSTANCES, someone would have heard. The Lagro house is in a subdivision carved out of the side of a hill, and although each house is built on its own little plot of land and surrounded by concrete walls, someone would still have heard something. The living room had been a wreck when Saenz, Rueda, and his team arrived; the bedrooms only slightly less. When she fell from the stairs, it was likely that she screamed. When her body hit the glass table, it had shattered on impact. Either of the two would have awakened someone.

But everyone WAS awake, and still nobody heard anything. A much bigger racket was drowning it all out. It was New Year's Eve when the killer came into her home, and nobody heard them battling it out above the din of firecrackers, blaring car horns, paper trumpets, random gunfire, and people shouting and singing in the streets. He could not have chosen a better time to strike.

Saenz is sure of one thing: She knew the man. She knew him, and she had let him in. She was polite. She made coffee. She served cookies. They talked, they drank. Somewhere between coffee and her neck breaking, something happened, an argument perhaps. He had flung her around the room, but she had flung him right back. She had been a strong woman, and she didn't make it easy for him. If a neighbor hadn't made an excess of potato salad for Media Noche, brought it over to share with Libby, taken the open gate as an invitation and the open front door as a warning, Libby's body might not have been found for days.

Saenz had taken a picture of her before they took her body away. His phone is filled with dead faces. He remembers each and every one of them, the ones he could help and the ones he couldn't. The faces are mostly slack and blank. Sometimes the fear is unmistakable, drawn plain in the wide eyes, the twist of the open mouth.

Her dead face is different, neither blank nor afraid. When he goes to bed he tries to forget it, but her face stays in his mind, hovering in the darkness there. Several times in the night he is compelled to look at the photograph. *Just one more time, this will be the last, I've got to get some sleep.*

He finally recognizes what's written on her face: not fear, but fury.

SHE'S FOURTEEN. SHE comes home from school one day, her mother is sitting on the kitchen floor. There's broken glass everywhere, shards of plates whose patterns she can still recognize.

She knows her mother will be sitting on the floor like this for a while. She takes a broom and a dustpan and begins to sweep carefully around the woman.

When they go shopping for new plates days later, the girl suggests to her mother, with deliberate nonchalance, that they buy plastic ones. "It's cheaper," she explains, and leaves it at that.

HER NAME WAS Olivia Delgado—Libby. She was thirty-nine, and she lived alone. She read a lot, and liked Jack 'n Jill potato chips (*twelve packs, three different varieties in the kitchen cupboard*). Libby didn't seem to have many friends, if her profile page on one of those social networking websites was anything to go by. She wasn't pretty, but in her pictures she looked straight into the camera, relaxed, confident, the barest hint of a smile on the corners of her mouth. She wasn't into sports but had climbed six mountains, wasn't much into clothes but had forty-three pairs of shoes.

Saenz wants to take aside and question the few people at her memorial service—relatives, friends, colleagues. But they recognize him from the television news; they know who he is and what he does for the police, and they actually go out of their way to avoid him. He finds this odd. He tells Rueda a few days later and Rueda grimaces.

"I thought you priests were trained to be sensitive. You didn't think it was a bad time to be asking questions?"

"I was trying to help," Saenz snaps.

"I know, Father. I didn't mean to—"

Saenz waves him away. "No, you're right. It was . . . inappropriate."

Rueda has known Saenz for decades. When he was younger, the priest used to be genial, easygoing. Over the years, however, he has grown quieter, more guarded. He still looks preternaturally younger than his age—Saenz in his sixties remains a showstopper of a man—but his eyes are ancient, haunted. He's prone to irritability and ill temper. It's difficult now for Rueda's younger officers to believe that the priest who comes to their crime scenes every once in a while ever used to be "a nice man." At best he's reserved; at worst he's testy and dismissive. And he's always in a rush, always telling people to hurry up. Age slows most people down, but then again Saenz isn't most people. If anything, age seems to have sped him up, downright turbocharged him, with little patience or understanding to spare for anyone who can't keep up.

Rueda thinks Saenz is racing to finish as much as he can, while he still can.

He slides a notepad across the table to the older man. There's a list scribbled on the top page. "I don't have enough people to do this, and I've got my hands full till Wednesday."

Saenz rips the page off and folds it neatly, slips it into his shirt pocket, makes for the door. He is grateful but he doesn't say anything. They know each other well enough that such niceties are no longer necessary.

SHE'S SIXTEEN, OLD before her time, and finally escapes high school. It's time for her real life to start, she's good at math, she chooses a major. She keeps everyone at bay because people are always asking questions she doesn't want to answer.

She's seventeen, she tries out for the swim team and makes the dean's list, her mother breaks and heals and breaks again. She's eighteen, she passes her driving test. She wants to wait for her father outside his office and run him down, back up and drive over him, again and again in a loop until there's nothing left of him but a stain on the concrete. It's a fantasy, she knows she can't do it, so she studies hard, she applies herself. She sees the future as a dark tunnel through which she must pass to get to the light, dragging her mother behind her.

She graduates with honors, gets three offers almost instantly and chooses the best, not the one that pays the most. She combs through real estate listings, claws her way to independence. She learns to climb mountains. She bides her time.

THE PEOPLE ON the list are cooperative. Which is a bit of a waste since they seem to know very little about Libby Delgado. Worked at a foreign bank, in a fairly senior position. Comfortable but not rich. Parents dead. No siblings. Bought the Lagro house a little over a decade before. Rented an apartment closer to her workplace but always spent the weekends in Lagro. Didn't employ a maid or any kind of household help. Kept to herself. The people on the list are perfectly helpful but also perfectly opaque.

Something itches in Saenz's brain, sly and relentless and maddeningly out of reach.

He asks to be let into her house again. Rueda comes with him. Everything remains as they had left it that New Year's morning. She had few relatives, and she wasn't very close to any of them. There has been no mad scramble for her worldly possessions, something rare in this part of the world.

Saenz walks through the house, muttering to himself. Rueda follows him around, careful not to distract him. The priest stops at a small utility room just off the kitchen, looks down at a small pile of clothing dumped on the floor beside the washing machine. *Odd.* Then he walks a little farther down to a tiny bathroom.

"Your boys dust in here?" he asks.

"Guest bathroom? Yes."

Saenz fully alert now, almost buzzing. "The coffee cups."

A beat, then Rueda understands. "You think he used the bathroom. You want to see if we can find a match."

"The living room was trashed, and the upstairs. But no other signs of struggle or disarray anywhere else." The priest moves back toward the washing machine, his eyes narrowing to focus on the pile of clothes on the floor. "Except in here."

He bends to pick up a blouse, and the rest of the small pile comes up along with it. He is momentarily confused and then he realizes that they're all still attached to a small, blue plastic clothes rack. Saenz carefully plucks through the clothing until he finds what he is looking for.

"Hook's broken."

Rueda comes closer. "So it was torn off the . . ." Saenz darts off before he can even finish, looking around for a pole or makeshift clothesline—anywhere the rack could have been hung from. He finally finds the broken-off plastic hook on the floor of the shower stall in the guest bathroom.

"It was hanging from the shower curtain pole," Rueda says, trying desperately to follow the priest's mental leaps. "You think he saw it when he used the bathroom. It set him off." He turns to Saenz. "But why?"

Saenz unclips the flimsy little blouse from the rack, holds it up by the shoulder seams. He tosses it on top of the washing machine, takes another tiny article of clothing from the rack. Pink T-shirt, held up, examined, tossed. Nude brassiere. Matching panties.

Finally, he looks at Rueda, those strange, light-colored eyes burning. He grabs the clothes with one hand, thrusts them almost in the police officer's face. "Libby Delgado was not a small woman."

SHE PUTS A down payment on the house on Caridad Street because the neighborhood is quiet, and there is greenery all around it; it's not far from the La Mesa

Watershed, the air is cleaner than elsewhere in the city. When she looks up at the night sky, she can see hundreds of stars.

She puts a down payment on the house because it is isolated and not easy to find. The house has high walls and a sturdy gate. It's in a part of the city that is still considered too far from the center of things. The area is underdeveloped; there are not many public transport options. People imagine that rapists and the ghosts of the unquiet dead lie in wait in the carabao grass grown tall and wild on the vacant lots that line its highways and streets. They're not too far wrong—a bloated body is dumped in the grass nearly every other month. It isn't until years later that the mega-malls set up shop, and developers start snapping up the land and property values shoot up. Most of the grass is cleared away but the ghosts linger.

She puts a down payment on the house and never tells anyone where it is, so that it will be easier to keep her mother safe. She's not much afraid of ghosts, but she knows that monsters are real.

"WE'RE ASSUMING SOMEONE else was staying with her. Another woman." Rueda hands the priest a mug of coffee, black and strong just the way he likes it. "Who was she? Was she there when Libby was killed?"

Saenz shakes his head. "It's not a big house. If someone else had been there, she would have been found, she would have been dragged into that massive struggle somehow. You have only two blood samples, Libby's and the killer's.

Highly unlikely that whoever owned those clothes was there when Libby died."

"Who, then? House guest? Lover?"

"Don't know." Saenz scowls into the liquid in his mug. "Don't know who Libby Delgado is, either."

"Sure we do, we—"

"No," the priest cuts him off sharply. "Don't fall into that trap, Mike. We know only what she wants us to know. We need to find out what she's hiding."

Saenz talks like she's still alive.

THE HOUSE CAN'T hold her mother; she eventually goes back to her husband, thinks that he can be saved, that this is what a good, strong Catholic marriage should be. It's funny-sad, when Libby thinks about it. She lost her own faith ages ago. God is dense, is deaf, is dead, is a one-trick pony, putting people on this earth only to forget about them.

The next time God forgets about them, she calls the police. Later, she calmly gives testimony. Her father is put away for a while, but he gets out soon after, slap on the wrist, that's just how it is. Her mother stays and stays. Libby tells her, *you can always come live with me. But you have to choose.* She almost says *you have to choose me.* But she doesn't, because it won't happen. And she cannot keep dashing herself over and over again on the jagged, treacherous rocks of her parents' lives.

She never speaks to them again. Cancer kills her mother before her father can, a minor miracle. She goes to the funeral but she stands way off in the background, where nobody can see her. When she gets home, she throws every photograph, every keepsake, every card and gift and letter—every single thing that reminds her of her family—into a box. Then she marches out into the backyard and sets the box on fire. She stands close, sticks a hand briefly into the licking flames to see how it feels: the bonfire of her history.

Watches it all burn.

LIBBY'S DESKTOP AND notebook computers are filled with spreadsheets, charts, graphs, and documents for work. When she surfed the internet, she checked the market indices, read newspapers, shopped for books and shoes. Her bookmarks included dozens of news websites, online booksellers, auction sites. She did not maintain a blog, did not keep a diary of her thoughts, at least not one that Saenz has been able to find. And although he can easily ask Rueda to find someone who could sniff out her electronic trail, hack into her emails, an acute sense of propriety prevents him from doing so. Her planner does not give him much to work with, either. Aside from meetings at work, she recorded little of her life, a few lunches and dinners, the occasional party.

But after thumbing through it for the fourth time, the priest notices something. There are appointments with people whose names she spells out clearly—*Vicki* and *Faye* and *Jorge*—and others where she only writes initials. It could be something, it could be nothing, but it's unusual. People often write a certain way and stick with it—names, dates, numbers. It becomes second nature, instinctive. To write full names for some and initials for others, it's a deliberate thing. *Why would you do that? Why don't you want us to know who you were meeting? AS and FJ and the last one, first appearing in late October, EV? Who were they?*

Her latest credit card statement arrives a few weeks after her death. Rueda forwards it to his office along with the rest of the mail, just bills and flyers. Saenz studies the document carefully. *You bought a plane ticket. Just four days before you died. Where were you going?* The thing that itches in his brain unfurls pale, gelid tendrils, coils them around its fat, glistening lobes.

He makes a telephone call to Rueda, and Rueda in turn makes a series of telephone calls to other people. A day passes, two days, three. On the fourth day Rueda calls back. The flight was headed to General Santos City on the morning of the thirty-first of December. But the ticket wasn't for Libby, it was for an Evangeline de Vera.

EV.

"Do we know who she is?"

"My people are checking."

"Call me when you know. Oh, and Mike?"

"Yes, Father?"

"We need to know if de Vera made that flight, and if she's back in Manila. And if not—we want her back."

THE FIRST TIME it happens, she surprises herself. She finds herself telling the woman sitting across from her (*colleague, twenty-six, married two years, miscarried once because of* *the beatings*) that she'll help. The words come out before she can censor them, before she can think about the implications. She lays down the ground rules, making them up as she goes along, realizing only much later that they make perfect sense. *Don't call him, don't meet with him in person, don't tell him where you are. Communicate only through your lawyer, the lawyer I'm going to introduce to you, he's a good man.* She lets her stay at the house in Lagro for a few weeks; when the time is right, she sends her away to a relative in another city, someone the woman trusts.

It's more than a year later when she receives word of the annulment from the woman herself; a telephone call, exhausted but happy, and so very grateful. It's a long conversation. After she hangs up, she breaks open a bottle of wine, puts on some Cole Porter—the *Classic Cole* album by Jan DeGaetani—and dances slowly in the living room in her bare feet.

It happens again, once, twice, word gets around. She forks out her own money, and if she doesn't have enough, she works the telephone and writes emails, she calls in favors, asks a few trusted friends. She seems to know instinctively how to do this, she becomes an expert, she could write a manual. She falls into it as though she were meant to do it, born to do it, weaving it seamlessly into the fabric of her life.

When her father dies, the relatives ask her to please come. She refuses but she says, *send me the urn.* When it comes, she drives to a run-down gas station along Regalado Avenue, heads for the restroom, locks the door. She empties the contents of the urn into a filthy toilet bowl and flushes them down the drain. And flushes. And flushes. And flushes.

THE WOMAN WHO knocks on Saenz's door is in her fifties, short and plump and well-dressed. He immediately pegs her for a teacher. *Come in,* he signals with a wave of his hand.

She seems nervous, and Saenz reminds himself to be gentle, *you remember how that goes, don't you?*

She is Professor Josephine Atienza, one of Libby's former teachers at the University of the Philippines. She says she read in the papers that Saenz was helping with the investigation. The words tumble out one after another, she keeps talking even as she puts her handbag in her lap and roots around in it for something. There's a certain desperation in her speech and her actions, as though she must get this business in his office exactly right.

When the professor finds the slip of paper that she is looking for, she pulls it out and hands it to Saenz. He reads what's written on it.

"Libby came to my office just after Christmas. She said she urgently needed a place to stay in GenSan. I was born and raised there, so she came to me. A short-term stay of a month or two. I asked her why GenSan of all places, and she said she was working on a project." Professor Atienza taps the paper with her forefinger. "That's the place I recommended."

Saenz studies the paper for a moment, then looks up at the professor. "She lied to you," he tells her.

Anger flickers in her eyes but it's quickly replaced by resignation, and she swallows down whatever she may have been thinking of saying. "Libby never lied. She just left out the truth."

THE WOMAN'S HUSBAND is Korean, and he is something of a sexual sadist. She wears a scarf at her throat, the bruises fading now from ugly purple to mottled yellow. She tries to explain the things he does to her in the bedroom, but she can't quite find the words because nothing in her life before him has prepared her for this, for the kind of assault he inflicts, for the level of filth he subjects her to, she has no vocabulary for it. She looks about ready to crawl out of her skin.

Libby sits back and listens to the woman try to tell her story in between great, racking sobs. At some point, she looks out the window, at the trees outside. She hasn't tuned out; she's just hearing the story in another woman's voice. After a while, all these women tell their stories in that same voice.

SAENZ USED TO think that when he got to this age, sleep would come more easily. Not true; or perhaps, just not true for him. He cannot remember the last time he slept seven or eight hours straight; it seems an impossible luxury. He stays awake for long stretches, sometimes longer than twenty-four hours. When he finally collapses from exhaustion, his mind struggles mightily against the tide of sleep. He snaps awake in an hour or less. It takes him another hour or two to fall asleep again, and the cycle starts over. He's always so tired, it's become an agony to put one foot in front of the other every day. Some days he feels tethered to the earth by the leaden weight of his own aging body, and he prays for release.

It's been several months now since they found Libby Delgado. Every day that passes, the man who killed her slips further away from their grasp. Lab tests, requests for information, paperwork, everything moves slowly, as it always does in Manila. Rueda tries his best, he always does, that's why Saenz likes him, but the system is what it is, it's like swimming in cold porridge. The DNA, the hair, the fingerprints don't match anything on record, but given the state of recordkeeping in the country, it was always going to be a long shot.

She pulls him into her gravity every night, even though there's nothing left of her but a few handfuls of ash in a marble jar somewhere. *Who are you?* he rasps out when he wakes from his fragmented dreams, his uneasy sleep. He reaches for his mobile phone, he can't help it, he's drawn to those eyes, so very angry, so very alive in her dead face.

THE GROUND RULES are clear. *No direct contact with him. Always through a lawyer, or the police if necessary.* It is the First Rule, a kind of detox to break his hold on the woman's mind and will. It gives her a chance to see through all the little tricks calculated to make her feel small and defective and unworthy. It forces her to start hearing her own voice and thinking her own thoughts again.

The Second Rule is: *if you break the first rule, you must never tell him where you are.*

FROM THE PENSION house on Pioneer Street in GenSan, Rueda's people manage to trace Evangeline de Vera to the home of a cousin in the same city. They bring her back to Metro Manila, and all the while she demands to know why. When they tell her, she is utterly stunned, she has no idea. She has had no access to Manila newspapers these last few months, and her cousin's family doesn't watch the news on television.

She and Libby have little in common, don't move in the same circles. Evangeline is in her late twenties, tiny, blandly pretty. Barely got past high school. Used to work as a waitress at a karaoke joint where she met the Korean businessman she eventually married. She has no children, no job.

Rueda asks Evangeline how she met Libby, why the older woman would buy a plane ticket in her name and pay for it with her own credit card. She says she hadn't known Libby very long, and she doesn't remember how they met. But she insists they were friends; she was short of cash for a sudden trip to see her family, and Libby was kind enough to lend her the plane fare and the money for her accommodations.

"But you're married. Why didn't you just ask your husband for the money instead?" Rueda probes.

Both the inspector and the priest—one inside the room, the other watching the exchange from outside—are quick to notice that brief moment of hesitation.

"He was . . . out of town." She won't look directly at Rueda. "Traveling."

Unnecessary, Saenz thinks. *People add unnecessary emphasis or detail when they're lying.*

When they take a break, Rueda asks him, "What if it's true? What if that's really all there is, and we're wasting our time?"

Saenz holds up both hands in the universal sign of *stop right there.* "She can't—won't—tell us how she met Libby. Who introduced them. Exactly how long they've known each other. Why she couldn't ask her husband for the money. She's being evasive. She's *terrified.*"

On a hunch, he asks Rueda to bring him Libby's planner and the clothes they found near the washing machine at her house. When they arrive, both men go back into the room where Evangeline is waiting. Rueda introduces the priest. The tension that ripples through her small frame is unmistakable.

Saenz sits across from her, and Rueda takes up a seat in one corner of the room.

The priest does not ask her questions. Instead, he tells her a story—her story—in his low, quiet voice, reading off dates and entries in the planner. He tells her that she met Libby at her office on the twenty-eighth of October last year. Someone named Gemma introduced them. They met again several times, without Gemma, but never again at Libby's office, always in a public place—a fast-food joint, a café, a park.

He tells her that she met Libby three times at a hospital,

first in late November and twice in December. He says that Evangeline was either sick or injured—the entries in Libby's planner switched from *meet* to *visit* the first two times, and to *pick up* on the third. He tells her gently that it would be relatively easy for the police to check on the circumstances of these hospitalizations. He tells her that Libby booked the flight and paid for it four days after *pick up EV from hosp.*

Evangeline is gripping the armrests of her chair so hard that her knuckles jut sharp and white through the skin of her hands.

Saenz draws the clothes out of the plastic bag they came in. "These are yours," he says, laying them on the table and pushing them across to her. "You stayed with her after you were discharged from the hospital. You left them to dry in the guest bathroom when you flew off to GenSan."

She reaches out and touches them.

"He found them," Saenz tells her quietly, sadly. "It made him angry."

"He couldn't have," she protests, confirming his theory without even realizing it. "How could he . . . Oh, God." There it is, the horror of it, coming to her now in all its unforgiving clarity. "I called him. She told me not to, but I thought it would—calm him down."

"And you told him where you were staying," the priest says.

Evangeline de Vera, breaking Libby's rules. "Oh God. Was it because of me? *Was it my fault?*"

The two men don't answer. To Evangeline, that's answer enough.

• • •

LIBBY ALWAYS MAKES it a point to lock herself away on New Year's Eve, because she can't stand the noise and the smoke. It's easier to do it in the Lagro house, up on a hill, and even though the neighbors will be setting off fireworks and drinking and generally making fools of themselves, their homes are far enough apart that she doesn't really have to suffer through any of it. She plans her own private celebration with a tub of ice cream in the fridge and a few action films on DVD.

She is about to lock the gate when the car drives up. When the man steps out, she immediately knows who he is and why he is there.

Libby knows that it isn't wise to engage him; he's calm now but she senses his anger, it's coming off him in waves. Quickly, she estimates how long it's been since Evangeline's plane took off, *twelve hours, that's enough time, if she follows instructions.*

But she hasn't, which is why he's here. And Libby thinks she might be able to buy Evangeline a little more time, so she shakes his hand, invites him in for coffee and some of those rosquillos that a colleague at the bank had brought her from Cebu.

Before they go into the house, she steals a look at the night sky. Between the New Year's Eve fireworks and the smoke now hanging heavy over the city, she can't see a single star.

• • •

THE POLICE HAVE learned that Hann Hyun-jun fled the country less than a week after Libby Delgado's murder. They've matched samples of his hair and fingerprints from the condo unit he had shared with Evangeline to the samples found in Libby's house. But there's little that can be done other than to get Interpol to put out a Red Notice for him and wait. He has money, though, and he could go anywhere. Rueda tells Saenz there's no way to tell how soon, or if, he will ever be found.

The priest continues to reconstruct Libby Delgado out of Evangeline de Vera's recollections, out of the connections that are now emerging from their association. They web out into the lives of other women—Fanny Jamora, Astrid Samaniego, Lisa Marie Borja. The list spans eight years, five cities, thirteen lives—nineteen if he counts the children. She took it all on herself, led by some impulse that even now eludes him.

She's left him little to go on with, and there's no family history to be found anywhere in the silent house on Caridad Street. But Saenz is patient, he wants to know—to understand her life and the magnitude of what she's done.

PROFESSOR ATIENZA MEETS him at the Starbucks café at the huge new SM Fairview mall along Quirino Avenue. She insists on buying him a coffee—his usual double-shot espresso, not helping the insomnia—and chooses for herself the sweetest, richest concoction on the menu, three hundred tablespoons of sugar and a half-pound of whipped cream. "Life is short," she declares. She giggles like a schoolgirl, guilty and defiant at the same time.

The mood changes once they're settled at a table; they sit in silence for several minutes, as if bracing themselves for what's to come. "You knew, didn't you?" he finally asks. "When you came to my office. You knew who was staying at the pension house in GenSan."

Tears gather in her eyes, and she fiercely blinks them away.

"I didn't know who. But I knew why."

Saenz leans forward, his pale, fine-boned hands clasped together in between his knees. In his mind, Libby's eyes slowly lose their anger, her face relaxing into the easy, barely there smile in the photographs that are not on his mobile phone.

"Tell me," he says.

ROAD TRIP

A beach, a grill, a beer, a birthday. The chief's birthday, always an important day for the team, and the sole reason for this trip. The pandemic lockdown wasn't even discussed during the planning. As far as the chief and his men are concerned, it's a nonissue.

The convoy has been on the move since the morning, and the beach resort is still two or three hours away. In Valles's car there are five men. He's the only one wearing a mask.

They stuck Valles in the seat with no window shade. The afternoon sun is merciless, and the men beside him are fast asleep, mouths hanging open, a pair of large, lumpy manspreaders, their bodies like tallow melting on the upholstery. Valles tries to make himself thinner in the space left to him. His legs are cramping, and he tries discreetly to rotate, first one foot, then the other, to get the blood flowing again.

Logronio, the driver, gives Valles a glance in the mirror. "Hoy, Valles. You'd better keep that stupid mask on, ha. I don't want your sour face spoiling our fun."

Valles adjusts the loops of the mask around his earbuds and turns up the volume on his music player.

Valles is startled awake when Logronio bangs on his

door. "Hoy, Sleeping Beauty." He eases himself out, limbs stiff.

The others have already piled out of their vehicles. They strut and preen in their cutoff jeans and sleeveless muscle tees, bellies hanging over their waistbands. An air of thuggish authority clings to all that wobbly bloat, even without uniforms.

The rest stop has ample dirt and gravel parking. An open-air carinderia stands at the back end of the property, attached to what looks like a run-down house. There's a row of restrooms off to one side.

There are five or six long tables, and seven or eight round ones for smaller groups of diners. But the plastic chairs are all stacked up beside a counter, its wood painted a curious burnt orange. On it stands a rusty cash register, probably dating back to the late eighties. A round clock with a plain white face hangs from the wall behind the counter. The wall is painted the same shade of orange.

The officers are the only ones there.

"Is it even open?" Valles asks no one in particular. He's not quite sure how the lockdown is observed this far out of Metro Manila, but it looks like the carinderia hasn't been in operation for weeks.

"They'll open for the chief," Logronio says.

The chief descends from the vehicle with a slight groan, and the gravel crunches loudly under his heavy feet. The other officers part to make way for him. "Oy, what are you waiting for? Tell them we're hungry."

A few of the men, including Logronio, rush to the

house and the carinderia, shouting, knocking on doors and windows. It's not long before a man and two women emerge. He's clothed in faded denim cutoffs and a tattered brown T-shirt. The older woman is wearing what looks like a matching pajama set, red polka dots set against a dingy white background. They're both gray haired, with missing teeth. The younger woman is in a pale pink housedress with cap sleeves and pockets, a row of tired ruffles circling her knees. Their makeshift masks can't hide the fear in their faces, in their eyes.

Valles catches a few words: *cook, dinner, pork, fish*. But he also catches the words *nothing, closed, family*.

As always, the violence seems to come out of nowhere, random, easy. Logronio reaches out to slam the man's head against the wall of the house. The women gasp and cower, and the man reels. Logronio grabs a handful of his hair and slams his head again, harder. This time there's a trickle of blood down the side of his face.

"Stop," Valles calls out. "Stop it."

"Shut up, Valles," Salvador hisses at him.

The chief just chuckles. "Such a Boy Scout, this Valles. You'll thank us when your belly is full tonight."

The older woman is weeping—Valles guesses she's the man's wife. But the younger one musters enough courage to steady her voice. "We can cook whatever we have at home for you. But it will have to be simple, because there hasn't been much at the market to buy these last few weeks."

Logronio releases the man so abruptly that he staggers back against the wall, and the woman rushes to her husband's side. Satisfied with himself, he pulls his shorts up toward his belly. As he moves away from the couple, he notices a battered old beverage refrigerator near the counter. "Hey," he says to the young woman. "Don't forget the beer. And make sure it's cold."

THE SUN HAS fully set by the time the man finishes cooking. His wife piles the food high onto large serving dishes: mounds of steaming hot rice, slabs of grilled pork belly marinated in soy sauce and calamansi, fried black tilapia. There are bowls of lowland vegetables—okra, eggplant, squash, and malunggay, simmered in a light fish broth until tender.

The young woman is setting tables: tattered plastic tablecloths in a faded blue-and-white check, chipped, rose-patterned plates—for some reason, it's always roses in carinderias like these. The green-tinted drinking glasses are sturdy, heavy-bottomed, scratched and cloudy from frequent use. She lights oil candles in the same heavy glasses, two or three at each occupied table, to keep insects away as well as to supplement the feeble yellow glow from the bulbs that hang from the rafters.

The officers crowd around the chief's table, eager to be close to the birthday boy. They'd proposed this spur-of-the-moment trip last night, never mind the lockdown, and he'd eagerly gone along with the plan, happy to get away from his wife and the sweltering city. He'd been promised a pretty girl—girls, even—when they got to the beach.

Valles sits by himself at a separate table. The young woman brings him a plate of food and a bowl of vegetables.

He looks up. The masks can't hide their expressions—his, apologetic; hers, angry. He removes his mask and thanks her quietly.

"Hoy, Valles," Logronio yells at him. "Thinking about dessert already, are you?" The other officers around him snicker at the innuendo.

The girl glances coldly at Logronio, tilting her head at an angle that seems almost unnatural to Valles. He looks away quickly, just in time to see the candle on his table flicker violently in its glass. It's a second or two before he realizes there's no wind.

She walks away without a word.

"Hala, you're not her type."

They all laugh raucously, as if on cue. Valles doesn't answer. He turns his body away from the group, focusing on the food in front of him. He tries not to think too much about the cost of the meal, the certainty that they're not going to pay the bill.

HE'S FINISHING THE last of the broth when Salvador, beer in one hand, drags a chair toward him and settles himself in it. He puts his feet up on the table and studies Valles's face thoughtfully, a lit cigarette dangling from one side of his mouth.

"I don't understand you," he finally says.

"Me? Why?"

"Well, you don't like the unit. You don't like any of us, including the chief. You don't even seem to like this job very much. And you certainly don't care that nobody likes you." Salvador blows a double column of smoke through his nostrils straight into the air. "Yet you're still here. And no sign you're going to quit anytime soon."

Valles stacks empty bowl on top of empty plate and arranges his fork and spoon neatly beside them. "Are you going to ask me a question, or do you just like looking at my handsome face?" It's a joke, of course; Valles has a face like a chopping board, flat, pale, almost rectangular in shape and proportion.

Salvador squints at him through a cloud of smoke, then stubs out the cigarette in the tiny pool of broth left in Valles's bowl. "You'll find this strange, but I happen to like you." Valles's father, long retired and even longer dead, had mentored Salvador as a rookie in the service. It's the only reason he treats Valles a notch better than all the others in the team do. "You're smart, and you think fast on your feet. Truth is, if I were ever caught in a shootout down some dark alley, I'd want you watching my back."

He rises to his feet, pulling up the waistband of his jeans. He's the only one in the team, aside from Valles, who doesn't have a paunch yet. "So consider this advice from a friend. You'd better watch yours."

He leaves the table, walks out of the carinderia and toward the bathroom stalls.

Loud, drunken laughter erupts from the other tables again, and Valles turns to look. The young woman is in the middle of the group of officers, and she's arguing with Logronio. She's increasingly agitated, the color rising from her neck to the apples of her cheeks where the top of her mask ends. "We've given you all our supplies, and now my family doesn't have any food left. We don't know when we can go out and buy again. And we have to pay the supplier for those beers. This is not enough."

Valles sees the purple bills in her hand: three hundred pesos as payment for the dinners and drinks of thirteen men.

Logronio just keeps laughing at her, pretending to tuck his clutch bag under his armpit to protect it from greedy fingers. "Hoy, don't charge me Manila prices for a probinsya meal." His delivery has the rest of the men, including the chief, in stitches.

He reaches out with his free hand, grabbing her in the crotch through the fabric of her dress. "I can give you more, but only if you try to be nicer to me." She tries to back away but now there are men behind her, beside her, a wall of flab and muscle blocking her retreat. He wiggles his fat hand underneath her as he says it, wiggles it fast and then jabs hard. The chief roars in approval, and so do the rest of the men, their laughter deepening, darkening into something foul and ugly.

When she pushes his hand away, the clutch bag comes flying out, striking her hard in the face. In seconds, her right check reddens, and blood starts beading beside her eye.

Random. Easy.

Practiced.

Valles glances at the old clock on the wall behind the cash register. It's 8:45 P.M.

The light from the bulbs intensifies, and the candles start flickering wildly. When she touches her cheek, her fingertips come away red. She looks at her hand for a moment, and before Logronio can dart away, she smears blood on his forehead.

The light bulbs dim, and then die out completely, at the same time that the candles go out.

Valles feels static in the air, a sensation that feels like crackling fury. He can hear the other men cursing, angry, confused, a little frightened. "Hey, turn on the damn lights," the chief booms, while someone in the group tries desperately to fire up a lighter that won't work.

Valles suddenly finds the woman standing beside him. "Are you all right?" he asks. "I can—I have bandages in my backpack."

She doesn't glance at him, doesn't even seem to have heard what he's just said. "We must be paid," she says quietly.

The lights suddenly come on again, and the candles flicker to life. Valles blinks, but the woman is back in the middle of the group, and he wonders how she could have moved so fast. This time her father and mother are holding her, leading her away, it's all right, dear, come away now, we're so sorry, of course this is enough, please just leave us alone.

Valles looks at the clock again. It's still 8:45. Must be broken. He checks his watch.

8:45.

The men start piling back into the vehicles. SUV doors slam shut, and Logronio yells, "Valles, you'd better get in here now or I'll beat you senseless."

Valles fumbles for his wallet and takes out a crisp thousand-peso bill. He clumsily holds it out to the father, who refuses to take it, then to the young woman, who just looks at him. A car horn bleats loudly, impatiently for him. He lays the bill on the nearest table and puts a glass on top of it so that it doesn't blow away, then hurries back to his vehicle.

"Damn you, Valles, next time we'll leave without you," Logronio says. There's a faint streak of blood on his forehead where she touched him.

"Just get in," Salvador tells him through clenched teeth.

Valles realizes there's blood on Salvador's forehead, too.

HE WAKES UP from a short but deep sleep and the first thing he hears is Salvador and Logronio arguing. "I told you to turn right here."

"Boss, we already made that turn."

"Where are we?" Valles asks, half yawning. "Are we lost?"

Before anyone can answer him, Baccay points through the windshield. "What's that?"

They look in the direction he's pointing. They see two lines of people walking slowly down the road perpendicular to theirs, all wearing white or black and carrying torches. "Looks like some kind of religious procession," Salvador says.

Baccay shakes his head. "That's not allowed. And look. No distancing." Valles finds this concern for the lockdown guidelines ironic, considering that they've been sitting in the SUV for hours, breathing in each other's exhalations.

The tone in Salvador's voice makes it plain that he's not interested. "Come on, Logronio, everybody's tired, let's just find that stupid resort." Logronio grunts, then makes a U-turn. The bigger SUV with the chief flashes its headlights and follows suit.

Even in the dim light of the SUV's interior, Valles can see there's a faint streak of blood on Baccay's forehead.

"There's, uh, some dirt on your face."

"Oh yeah?" Baccay fishes a bunch of table napkins swiped from the carinderia out of his pocket. "Where?"

"Forehead," Valles says, and looks away. He checks his watch: 8:45. Is it broken?

"Thanks."

He hears the soft rustle of the tissue paper rubbing against Baccay's forehead, then glances at the clock on the dashboard: 8:45.

"What time is it?" he asks.

Salvador checks his phone. "8:45. Why?"

"Look, there they are again," Baccay says.

Dimaano, who's been in a beer-induced stupor since they left the rest stop, is finally awake. "Who?"

"The procession," Valles says. Two rows of people, dressed in black or white, walking slowly, carrying lit torches. "But that's really strange. How could they have gotten to this end of the road so fast?"

Salvador is annoyed. "Has to be a different group. Either that or Logronio here has been driving us around in circles."

"What's the name of this street?" Valles asks.

"So many stupid questions," Logronio shouts. "Just shut the hell up."

"Sign says Hermana Mayor," Dimaano says, pointing to a street sign near a lamppost. "Corner Achuete." As the light catches his face, Valles sees the same streak of blood on Dimaano's forehead.

"Okay, you were supposed to turn right at Achuete," Salvador tells Logronio, exasperated. "Can you just follow the damned Waze, please."

"What do you think I've been doing all this time?" Logronio gives the steering wheel a vicious turn, and they lurch violently onto a side street. If not for his seat belt, Valles would have slammed into the back of Logronio's seat.

"Easy, easy," Baccay says.

Valles looks out the rear windshield—the larger SUV is following not too far behind them.

When he was a child, he'd lived through a typhoon so bad that it carried off, first his family's roof, then his family's home, then half of his family. When the terrible howling of the wind finally ended after two or three hours, he'd come out of his hiding place under the kitchen sink, dazed. He moved slowly, walking barefoot over shards of broken glass and tile and splintered wood. There were a few other people walking around just like him. They, too, were slow, confused, as though they'd all just woken up from a deep sleep and found themselves in another place.

He couldn't recognize his neighborhood, his street. All the homes and structures had been leveled; all the trees snapped like twigs. He'd never seen so much of the sky, gray and naked and sprawling. And the silence that lay over everything—even louder than the howling wind, so loud, so electric that he'd had to clap his hands over his ears several times to make it stop.

That's what he's hearing right now, as they drive through this deserted street. It feels to him like they've been plucked out of time and dropped in the middle of this loud, crackling silence.

"Hey, this is a pretty long street, huh," Dimaano says idly. No one responds. To Valles, it seems that the farther along this road they go, the wider the gap between streetlamps and the dimmer the light from them. Seconds, minutes tick by, and the road goes on and on.

"Oh, look," Baccay says, pointing once again to something not too far away. "Is that another procession?"

There it is, at the end of the road, two rows of people dressed in white or black, marching slowly, their faces blurred in the flickering light of the torches. "What the hell is going on," Salvador says impatiently. "It's not some kind of local holiday, is it?" He slaps Logronio's arm. "Get over there and ask them what's happening. And see if they know the way to the resort."

Logronio glares at Salvador. "Why me?"

"For once, will you do what you're told?" Salvador glances over his shoulder. "Valles, you go with him."

Logronio hits the brakes, kills the engine, and grudgingly leaves the vehicle, slamming the door. "Hoy, Valles. Don't say anything stupid, ha. Or else you're going to get it from me."

Valles knows better than to say anything when the other

man is in this mood. He follows a few paces behind him, his shoes crunching down on the fine gravel littering the road, and they approach the procession.

It's so quiet. Everyone in the procession is so quiet.

"Hoy," Logronio shouts. "HOY. What's happening here? What are you all doing?"

When the people turn to look at them, Valles feels a scream bubble up in his throat.

It's the man from the rest stop, and his wife, and their daughter. Many of them. *All of them.*

He looks at Logronio, who's still shouting, although Valles can't understand what he's saying anymore. "We have to go," Valles insists, and he can hear his voice trembling. "Come on, Logronio, we have to leave. Now."

Logronio snaps at him angrily. "Shut up, Valles," he says, glaring at Valles like he always does but with eyes now completely clouded over. The speck of blood on his forehead has turned to a thick but steady stream, black like tar and glistening in the light of the torches, flowing down the side of his nose, over his lips, staining his teeth. The "s" in Valles's name comes out a long hiss, and the air it expels with it forms a small black bubble on his lower lip.

The people are coming closer to Logronio now, listening, intent, so very focused on him, their hands reaching out, touching his arms, his hair, his groin, giving it a wiggle and a shake and several hard jabs. But Logronio's unperturbed, like everything is normal, like everything is as it should be, in his world where he is king and so very used to people being afraid of him.

It's the last thing Valles sees before the flames from the torches flicker out.

He turns and runs, stumbles, picks himself up, runs back to their vehicle. He opens the door on the driver's side, and he yells at Salvador, "We have to get out of here now."

The girl from the rest stop is sitting in Salvador's place. Valles looks at the back seat, and Baccay and Dimaano are not there. But her parents are.

The girl puts something on the driver's seat and slides it closer to him. It's his thousand-peso bill, stained with something dark and sticky from Logronio's fingers, stubby on the fat hand he used on her, now separated from the rest of him.

"We will be paid," she says quietly.

The digital clock on the dashboard says 8:45 P.M.

Valles lets go of the door handle like it's burning hot and backs off, slowly at first. Then he runs, runs as fast as his long stick legs can carry him. He runs to the second SUV, yelling for the chief and for the other men in it. But the doors and the windows are open, and the faces staring out at him are those of the man, and his wife, and their daughter.

He staggers backward, and bumps into someone. When he turns around, it's the chief, grinning at him with stained teeth, his eyes milky.

"Happy birthday to me!" he sings cheerfully, a syrupy blackness dripping down his chin. "Happy birthday to me!"

Valles feels a hand on his shoulder. He whirls around and it's Salvador, so close to him that he can smell something old and putrid on his breath. "Don't you worry, Valles. I've got your back."

He pushes Salvador away, and he runs, and he keeps running, down the long road and into the dark, as far away from that loud, howling silence as he can.

WHEN HE WAKES up, he's in a moving vehicle, bright sunlight shining through an open window. He sits up quickly and hits his head on the roof.

"What is this?" he says in a panic. "Where am I?"

There's a middle-aged man sitting across from him in what looks from the inside like a beat-up Toyota Tamaraw. He's wearing old swim goggles on the top of his head, a face mask, and plastic gloves. His eyebrows are the same wiry gray as his hair, his skin wrinkled, brown, leathery, his eyes kind.

"Take it easy. You were in an accident. Some folks found you, not far out of Mauban." He offers Valles a bottle of water. Valles ignores it. The man sounds almost apologetic. "You were in a car that fell down a ravine. And there was another car, too."

Valles asks where the others are—the chief, a dozen others.

The man holds out the water bottle again, but Valles waves it away. "We're not sure. We only found you."

"I want to go back. Take me back to where you found me. I need to see what happened."

"Look, we're supposed to take you to the nearest hospital."

"I have to go back. Take me back, now." He sees something familiar in the passing landscape, and lunges toward an open window. "Wait. I know this area. Please tell the driver to stop here. There's a rest stop not too far from here. Please, stop."

The man, confused, calls out to the elderly driver to stop. Valles frantically tries to unlock the door, and stumbles out of the Tamaraw, his legs rubbery. He runs to where the main entrance to the rest stop was, but the stone walls have crumbled and the land is overgrown with tall, wild grass, weeds, prickly bushes.

"We were here. Just last night." He moves forward and his chest tightens. There is no carinderia, no house, no restrooms, no parking lot: only a deep, gaping hole in the earth where all these structures should have been, and a foulness hanging in the air, like sewage, like rot.

"Hey, you watch out," the man in the back of the Tamaraw warns him. "Might be snakes in there."

"But we were here last night," Valles repeats, his voice breaking from the strain, his hands gesturing wildly in the direction of the empty lot. "They cooked for us. There was a house. There were tables and chairs. And an old refrigerator full of beer."

The man and the driver exchange glances. Valles immediately recognizes that they know something he doesn't, and that makes him even more desperate. "Look, I'm not lying. There was a family here. A man and a woman, and their daughter. Logronio—one of the officers I was with—he made them cook for us. There was a carinderia, and there were toilets for travelers."

"There hasn't been anything on that lot for the past

thirty, forty years," the driver says, wrapping his arms around the steering wheel and gazing straight ahead, as if avoiding having to look in the direction of the lot. "Family that owned the place got driven out by the police. Some big shot politician wanted to develop this whole area into a fancy subdivision."

Valles is trembling so hard, he can hardly suck air into his lungs. "Where did they go?"

"Nobody knows. But the developer ran into all sorts of bad luck here. Typhoons out of season, workers injured. Heard the big shot's wife caught some bad disease. Rotted her liver and lungs so bad they had worms when they opened her up." The old man leans out of the open window on his side, and spits on the ground. "They gave up on this old place soon enough."

He turns back to look in the direction of the carinderia. "But I was here. And they were here, too," he whispers, and now he's not trying to convince anyone anymore, only himself.

The old driver clicks his tongue. "Can't stay here long. We're supposed to get you to the hospital. We'd better get moving."

Valles walks slowly toward the Tamaraw, climbs aboard and shuts the door firmly behind him. The man holds out the water bottle for him, and this time, he accepts. The Tamaraw lurches forward, away from that deep hole, that wild grass, that reek of decay.